Quick Change

Also by Michael Kardos

Fiction
One Last Good Time: Stories
The Three-Day Affair: A Novel
Before He Finds Her: A Novel
Bluff: A Novel
Fun City Heist: A Novel

Nonfiction
The Art and Craft of Fiction: A Writer's Guide

Quick Change

Stories

Michael Kardos

Press 53

Winston-Salem

Press 53, LLC
PO Box 30314
Winston-Salem, NC 27130

First Edition

Cover art, nineteenth century magician poster
in public domain

Library of Congress Control Number
2026930340

ISBN 978-1-968783-02-0

for Katie

Grateful acknowledgment is made to the following publications where these stories first appeared:

Reality TV – *Cincinnati Review* (reprinted in *The Pushcart Prize XLVI*)

The Wish – *One Story*

Quick Change – *Ellery Queen Mystery Magazine*

Hero – *Blackbird*

America, Etc. – *One Teen Story*

Star to the East – *Swamp Pink* (formerly *Crazyhorse*)

Animals – *Swamp Pink* (formerly *Crazyhorse*) (reprinted in *The Pushcart Prize XXXIX*)

The Highest Point in Delaware – *Fiction International*

A Vanishing Story – *Unloaded: Crime Writers Writing Without Guns*

Mediation – *Swamp Pink* (formerly *Crazyhorse*)

Training – *Washington Square Review*

Contents

Reality TV

I was feeling nostalgic the other day while talking to my wife about the malls of New Jersey. I was surprised she didn't remember the Woodbridge Mall, the one with the tigers. She'd grown up in Wilmington, Delaware, but that wasn't so far away.

"The TV show?" I said as a memory jog. Nothing. So I told her how the Woodbridge Mall had been sprawling and adequate, not fancy like the Menlo Park Mall two miles down Route 1 with its posh anchor stores and food court full of healthy choices. For the holidays, the Menlo Park Mall went all out: enormous tree in the atrium, tens of thousands of lights, fake snow, the works. A carousel was brought in special for the season. Track laid all the way from Nordstrom's to Lord & Taylor for a train driven by an elf. *Toot toot* went the little engine.

The Woodbridge Mall couldn't compete with that level of family-friendly extravagance, so they went in another direction. They found twelve volunteers, chosen for their neediness and grit, and gave them all an hour together in the mall. For those sixty minutes, every item was free, theirs for the taking. They had only to carry the items they wanted to one of the exits. For these twelve people, this was a game changer. Maybe a life changer. This year, there would be gifts for their families, gifts for themselves, thank-you gifts, gifts of apology, gifts that spoke of every shade of human connection. Gifts to hock later for cash, if cash was their primary concern. No one would judge. For sixty minutes, everything was theirs. It would be the merriest of Christmases. The happiest of New Years.

"Except," I reminded Carly, "for the jewelry in the department stores. That was off-limits."

"Too expensive?" she asked.

"Maybe. I think it was more about making good TV." I remembered the contestants frantically dragging luggage and kitchen appliances and furniture and designer suits and dresses. Way more visually compelling than jewelry in the pockets.

"I guess that makes sense," my wife said.

Also during that hour, twelve half-starved Bengal tigers were set loose in the mall.

Obviously, this proposition wasn't for everyone. But the twelve contestants were willing and ready to shop, to appear on TV, and, they hoped, to avoid the tigers. They had signed the release forms and were determined by the show's team of physicians to be in acceptable physical condition.

"Seriously? None of this is ringing a bell?" I asked my wife. There weren't even many shows like it back then.

"So, people really got eaten on live TV?" she asked.

"It was taped, not live," I told her. "And it was all tastefully edited. They knew where to draw the line, editing-wise."

"But people got eaten?"

"Honey, these were hungry tigers in a mall." I remembered being a kid, my family together on the sofa, bowl of popcorn, rushing through homework during the commercial breaks. At first the tigers had trouble running on the hard floor. Their claws, designed for the grassy plain, had nothing to grip. Their legs would tangle and slide out from under them. This was played for comedy: the editors added a cartoony *whoop-whoop-SPLAT* sound effect. Soon, though, the animals got the hang of it. They'd crouch and creep, sniff their new territory. They'd pace and snarl. Dozens of mounted cameras throughout the mall gave the editors plenty to work with. The show's host drove a golf cart fitted with iron bars. He rode around and narrated in an excited whisper while a cameraman beside him shot footage. "I think Anita from Sayreville has her sights on the GE microwave oven with the rotating dish and automatic pizza setting." Or he'd spot a tiger and whisper something like "I'll tell you what, that tiger looks like he wants more than a bologna sandwich."

The show, *Malled*, ended after just nine episodes. During the taping of the last episode, all the contestants banded together and murdered a tiger. Then they kidnapped the host and tied his cameraman to a metal bench to show they weren't messing around. They looked right into one of the mounted cameras and said, "This is bullshit. Look what poverty and desperation have done to us." They demanded passports and plane tickets and money wired to an overseas account. They demanded safe passage. The tigers ate the cameraman. The cops moved in and shot three contestants.

The audience hated it. It's a game show, they complained. The contestants knew what they were getting into. They had no business getting political.

And I know. It seems like a long time ago, back when children gathered in person for school. Back when the government ran the national parks. Back when radiation levels east of the Mississippi allowed entry. Back when there were shopping malls. Back when there were tigers. Back when you could find a microwave oven. Before the Ten-Thousand-Year Flood and the Accident and the invention of the quickbullet. Before the Freedom Rampage. Before Crowdscatter. Before anyone had ever heard of the NX250-virus. Back when airplanes. Back when passports.

But it wasn't so long ago. I still remembered the one couple on the show, how they raced for the exit together, clutching each other, each one also holding a floor lamp, the cords dangling behind. Telling this to my wife, I touched my monitor and she touched hers, and it was almost as if there were no Great Quarantine and she and I were in a room together—truly, the same space. Almost as if we were holding hands.

The Wish

I've never been hit in the face, and neither have you. That was my thought, reading the poetry manuscript submitted by this writer and endowed professor of English with the mile-long CV.

In the opening poem, the speaker is punched by his next-door neighbor over the matter of dead tree limbs and who bore the responsibility for their removal. This got me thinking about all the people in books and movies and on TV who get punched in the face, and how this had never happened to me or to anyone I knew, except for one friend in college who, walking down the street, was sucker-punched by a man dressed in rags and muttering nonsense and probably flying on some drug or another. A cop saw it happen. The arrest took two seconds. In court several months later, the man looked sober, well-groomed, with a suit on. My friend couldn't even say for sure if it was the same guy. He wasn't after retribution anyway, my friend. The punch hadn't fully connected and had only turned his lip purple and loosened one tooth that tightened again on its own within the week. Point being, I wasn't in the mood to read any more poems by this professor who probably had no better understanding than I did about what it was like to be punched in the face, or the metaphor that best expressed the experience, or the childhood memory it conjured up, or the epiphany it brought about, or how the assault related to our current political situation. So I wasn't unhappy when Haley, the good summer intern, tapped on my door, forcing me to set down the manuscript and look up, squinting. The sun through my office window was relentless in the afternoon.

Haley's head poked through the doorway. "There's someone here to see you?" she said. "She said she has an appointment."

I looked at the time on my computer. The appointment wasn't for another half hour. I followed Haley into the reception area, which was just a larger office for our managing editor and the two interns.

The woman was about my wife's age. She had on a gray skirt and a white sleeveless shirt, and looked relieved when I gave her hand something to do by shaking mine. We introduced ourselves by our first names, and I led her to my office, where we sat and quickly got to the heart of things. There was no need to rehash what I already knew from the letter I'd received a week earlier—two pages of neat, error-free handwriting. I knew she must have polished it ahead of time and re-penned it before sending it to me. In the letter, she told me about her daughter's love of poetry, and about the disease for which there was no cure. Her daughter would die soon or, maybe, a little later than soon.

"I want to help," I told this woman now. Her name was Amanda Sims. "I think we can."

Amanda's eyes weren't shot through with red. They stayed dry even as she nodded. She was a thin woman with well-defined arm muscles, and I couldn't help thinking that she would need them. Soon she'd be lifting, carrying, supporting. She'd become a more physical being than she had probably ever been since first becoming a mother.

"I'm very grateful," she said.

I tried to smile appropriately. In the last year, I had too often been the recipient of the well-intentioned smile that failed to console. I wanted to convey sympathy and warmth, but not pity and definitely not hope.

"Tell me about Emma's poems," I said.

She opened her black shoulder bag and removed a manila envelope, from which she slid out a sheaf of paper.

"You decide which books to publish?" She glanced around my office. I kept it tidy: plant watered, photographs arranged, books alphabetized. Poetry volumes are thin, and if you don't shelve them properly you can spend your whole life tracking one down.

"I do," I said, and gave her a brief history of Pearce Books: founded in 1948 by the oil executive Clayton Pearce, who'd made a fortune pulling crude out of the Gulf of Mexico. Over the years, we'd maintained our niche as a small but important literary house, publishing about thirty books a year—poetry, fiction, some memoirs, the occasional work in translation. My tenure at the press was going on its twenty-third year. By now, I was the institutional memory.

"I don't know anything about publishing," she said. "But I knew you guys were based here, so I thought, why the heck not?"

"I'm glad you reached out." I looked down at the poems that Amanda had handed me, and for her sake I took a moment to read the first one to myself. It was called "Sea of Tears."

it is dark here
in all the salty water
the shore so far away
i kick but get nowhere

Which was more or less what I was expecting. I passed my eyes over the rest of the poem and made a show of paging through more of the manuscript. Then I set the pages down on my desk and rolled up my sleeves. "We can make a nice-looking book," I said. "Chad, our designer, is amazing." I told her I felt confident that my staff would jump right on this. "We could have a book-release party if Emma's up to it."

The mother shook her head. "No, that wouldn't be a good idea. We wouldn't want to do that."

"All right." I didn't want to make this woman get into details she'd rather not mention.

"I know we haven't talked cost," she said. "My husband and I discussed this, and we're willing to pay whatever—"

"Not necessary. We don't ask our authors to pay."

"All right. Thank you." For a moment her face brightened; then it dimmed again. "And how soon," she began, "if I may ask..."

I spared her the need to fumble though the rest of her sentence. "Two, three weeks?" I watched her eyes for signs as to the appropriateness of this timetable.

She nodded. "And you don't need to—" She looked around at my book-crammed office. "Check with anyone? Have a meeting or something? I mean, this can really happen?"

I was touched by how, despite the tragic circumstance, she sounded like every first-time author I ever gave the green light to. She didn't smile, but her eyes did. She was very pretty, and for the first time in months I caught myself noticing a woman's beauty. No: for the first time in months, I caught myself noticing beauty without feeling ashamed. I admired the fullness of her face, the flicker in her eyes. I considered, for a moment, telling her about my own recent loss but decided there was no utility in sharing this, not for her. It was enough that I knew. I felt that I was in a special position to feel the full force of the daughter's wish, which was also the mother's wish.

"Amanda, your daughter wants to see her book in print," I said. "I don't have a lot of power in this world, but I'm honored to be in a position to do this."

And now her smile entailed more than just her eyes. "Emma will be so excited—and her book will be in all the stores?"

I didn't follow. "Sorry?"

"Her book. Will it be everywhere?"

It's easy to forget how little most people know about book publishing. I realized I had gone too fast. "We're talking about turning your daughter's poems into something that looks like a real book, printing up copies—"

"No." She was shaking her head. "That isn't Emma's wish. Her wish is to be a published author."

"Sure," I said. "That's why we'll make it look—"

"No. Not *make it look*." She suddenly appeared stricken. "Emma wants to have a *real* book. Not a pretend one."

I'd recently read about a Make-a-Wish kid who'd been Batman for a day. "The boy who wanted to be Batman," I said to Amanda. "He didn't become the real Batman."

"*Sean*." Her voice turned sharper and a half-octave lower. I realized I hadn't been reprimanded for a while. "There *is* no real Batman, and that boy was a child." She turned her body to face the window and wiped her eyes with her hand. "I'm so sorry. I'm—" She stood up and reached across my desk, taking back her daughter's poems. She struggled to shove the pages into the manila envelope, which she put back into her bag. Then she rifled through her bag some more and came out with a small rectangle: a wallet-sized photo she dropped onto my desk.

"That's her," she said. "That's Emma. That's the face of my daughter."

The girl looked like her mother. Lighter hair, thinner face, teeth so straight her braces had maybe been removed that very hour.

"Amanda—" I began, but I wasn't sure what I might say after that.

"*What*?" She was glaring at me.

"Being in bookstores—that's not important." I tried to explain that even major poets don't have their books in "all the stores" the way she probably imagined. Poetry was a minor seller, and most bookstores devoted little shelf space to it. There were so many gray areas of publishing these days: self-publishing, print-on-demand, micro print runs. Ultimately, I told her, what made a book "real" was when the author believed it to be so.

She hadn't left my office, a good sign. "We won't list it in our catalogue," I said, "but her book will have a barcode so retail stores can order it and sell it. We can copyedit it this week and get the designer started."

She watched me, not answering.

"Amanda, I spoke too hastily before. Okay? It will be a real book."

"Just so I understand: you're saying if Emma tells someone her book is being published, she'll be telling the truth?"

The whump-whump sound coming through the wall was my associate publisher, Paul, walking on his treadmill that ran beneath his stand-up desk. He couldn't fire me because I was his boss. But he could kill me.

"The book will be real," I said.

Paul Mendez was fifteen years my junior. Ivy League grad, varsity squash, econ major who'd taken a fiction workshop his senior year, just for kicks, and it did him in. While his buddies became investment bankers and made a few fortunes apiece, Paul went on for an MFA and, afterward, took a job here as an editorial assistant. That was seven years ago. He swore he only regretted his life choices when he was on his yearly golf outings with his old college buddies, when they all went out for outrageous dinners and split the bill evenly, *for simplicity*, despite Paul's ordering nothing but a couple of appetizers.

Suffice it to say he didn't want to hear about my bad knees when we played racquetball at the gym. He was that way as an editor, too—not heartless, but ruthless. And intense. And a little heartless. He'd cut a manuscript in half, work a sentence until it begged for mercy. His authors complained bitterly and then won awards.

He and I played occasionally before Rose got sick, and more recently I'd been meeting him at the gym after work a couple of days a week because apparently my core was weak and that was the key to everything. Today, I told him, I'd rather drink.

"This mother?" Paul said after I told him what'd happened earlier. "She needs to understand reality a little bit."

"I doubt reality is the issue," I said. "I think she's enduring the worst reality she's ever known."

We were at the Blue Tavern, which had been a favorite spot of mine back when I had favorite spots. Rose would meet me here when she was done at the middle school, and we'd sit together and drink a beer. Nothing is better than talking about your day with your love at your favorite bar. I hadn't set foot in here in almost a year, since the day before the day when her oncologist first uttered the word "pancreas." But the city we lived in was too small, with too few good places to write one of them off permanently.

Paul was drinking a Perrier; I was down to the dregs of my second Old Fashioned. I hadn't drunk at all in Rose's last months, that surreal time of vigilance, of double- and triple-checking dosages, managing appointments, keeping the house clean, the refrigerator stocked with things she might eat or drink, helping her move about the house without falling, dealing with the insurance company, the various agencies, the homecare and nursing companies, with short-term disability and long-term disability and hospice. I'd been a caffeine-fueled, nervous insomniac too terrified of forgetting something important to risk even a light beer.

"If some dying kid wanted to pitch for the Cardinals," Paul said, "it would be staged. The game wouldn't *count*."

He was right, of course, But after Amanda had left my office, I couldn't resume work. Her perfume lingered. Her daughter's photo lingered. "We'll do a tiny print run," I told Paul, "make it available at Books and Cakes, donate any sales—"

He was tilting his head at me. "You already agreed to this, didn't you?" When I didn't answer, he said, "I just have to ask it—what do you think Rose would say?"

Rose—*Rose Petal*, always, to her mother; *Rosie B*, often, to me; *Rose Bennet, M.A.Ed* on her correspondence with parents—had been a phenomenal poet whose only fault had been placing too high a premium on the evils of nepotism. She knew from the moment we met that I could help her career, and she went to absurd lengths for me not to do so.

That was, from first to last, our one sticking point. She never understood that people *want* to help talented people. It's why editors become editors—to help talent get recognized. But Rose was a purist's purist. She let me read her finished work and on rare occasions asked me to weigh in with an editorial eye, but I wasn't allowed to help her professionally in any way. She wanted success, when it came, to be something she could trust—"to be real," in her words. She submitted her work only to contests that read anonymously, with the author's name omitted from the manuscript. For years she did this, and then she became sick, and then she died.

"I think Rose would have tremendous sympathy for a dying child," I told Paul.

"Sure," he said. "I also think she would tell the girl's mother to get a grip."

At home later, I sat on the back stoop beside a glass

of Makers Mark and got suitably drunk while the sky purpled and the bats dived for mosquitoes. A whole season had passed since Rose died. How was that possible? Sometimes I could almost imagine she was in the next room.

I went into the kitchen and sat at the table with my glass and Rose's third and last completed poetry manuscript, *Flame Waltz*. Like the first two, it was unpublished. I knew every page, had entire poems memorized. The manuscript wasn't broken into sections the way her first two had been. She finished it soon after the diagnosis and before her first round of chemo, when we were being told, It's serious, yes, but you have every reason to be optimistic. So we were. Rose had just turned forty, and even though we had decided long ago not to have children, for two weeks she gave serious thought to freezing her eggs. *Once this is all behind us*, she explained to me, *I mean, who knows, right?*

As for me, I vividly remember standing beside Rose that year over a chocolate birthday cupcake with a candle sticking out and feeling like I was betraying her physicians—their training and talent and years of experience—by casting birthday-cake wishes.

This last manuscript began with an epigraph.

> *"Grace / to be born and live as variously as possible"*
>
> *— Frank O'Hara*

I leafed through the pages. Eighty-two of them, the poems held together less by theme or form than by a more fundamental psychic glue. No sections this time because she wanted the manuscript to be messy, more like life. She hadn't really wanted children. That confession came a few months later. Freezing her eggs, it was just a passing thought, she told me. *I panicked. I thought maybe kids made you immortal.* By then, my most ardent wish had been downgraded to long remission. Then, later, to any remission. Then for it just to slow the fuck down a little. Then comfort.

One night about six weeks before she passed, we were on the sofa after dinner. (My dinner; she rarely ate anymore. Her appetite was gone and smells bothered her. I stopped making coffee in the house, and anything with garlic, and switched to scent-free laundry detergent.) I caught her reflection in the window, and in that brief, unexpected silhouette I saw her, and I saw the lack of her, all the weight she'd lost, and how little those Ensures I kept begging her to drink—doctor's orders—were doing, and I said to her, please, would she please let me publish the damn book? Her third manuscript was her best. I knew it was, and I told her so.

"And don't forget, it's my *job* to know." I smiled, trying to make light of a very serious request.

We almost never argued and rarely said an unkind word to each other. But that night she looked at me and said, "I know you've given up on me, you son of a bitch."

Had she lived, I believe she would have gone on to publish many books. Eventually, it would have happened. In my three decades of reading and editing manuscripts for a living, I'd come to conclude that talent in a writer was important but ultimately less so than perseverance. Rose had both, and once I became acquainted with her work and her work ethic, I never doubted that her first book would find a home—or, when she decided to set that manuscript aside, her second. I told her as much, repeatedly, and she must have believed me, and believed in herself, because for years she kept on driving those manuscripts to the post office. When technology changed and with it the submission process, she kept uploading anonymous files to prospective publishers. Season after season, year after year she did this with a learned, earned blend of dispassion and hope. We both knew not to take rejection personally. Some of those poetry contests received a thousand submissions and published only one. The odds are brutal, and at a certain point it comes down to dumb luck: your manuscript catches the right editor on the right day.

But I could have improved her chances. I could have played matchmaker, given her options beyond the anonymous contests. I could have put her manuscript on the desk of editors who wanted the type of poetry she wrote. I tried to explain that the real beneficiary of my involvement wouldn't be her, but her editor.

Rose held fast, and in time my frustration gave way to reluctant admiration for her perseverance. The flaw in my thinking—in both of ours—was not grasping that for perseverance to pay off, you have to live long enough.

Watching my thin wife's reflection in the kitchen window on the night she decided I'd given up on her, I decided that, in fact, Rose's perseverance was her worst trait. It was arrogant and unattractive. It was amateurish. It was nothing but repackaged fear.

I kept those thoughts to myself as she stood and walked to the base of the long staircase to our second floor. Leaning on the banister, she placed a foot on the first step, then the other foot. I knew better than to help, I had learned that several times over, and so I watched from my chair. But I could see that her days of stair-climbing were numbered. In the living room, already waiting for her, was a hospital bed that we pretended not to notice, as if we were a couple of Serengeti lions unable to see the tourist-filled jeep in front of them because it didn't belong to their world.

She kept writing until the last two weeks of her life, though she no longer let me read what she wrote. I was amazed that she could write at all, with all the oxycodone and methadone in her. Then one day she put the notebook aside and told me to promise to destroy all her manuscripts.

"My writing is a total meaningless failure. I'm

mortified for wasting so much of my time on it," said my best friend, my darling, my dying, drug-addicted wife. "You have to burn all of it."

"I can't burn your poems, Rose."

"Then recycle them. And erase my hard drive. You have to swear you'll do that."

"Come on. . ."

By then the hospital bed had become part of our world, had become the center of it. When she lifted her head, the cords in her thin neck stiffened. "You are *not* going to do anything with my manuscripts. They're mine. I need your word. I swear, I'll add it to my will if I have to."

She knew me too well. An idea had started to percolate in my head to publish her work posthumously. If not at my publishing house, then someplace else. The work deserved it: certainly her third book and probably the others, too. There were editors—not the half-formed MFA students who read for the contests she submitted to, but real editors of poetry—who, I believed, would be glad to have her work.

I told her she didn't have to change her will. She lowered her head again. I couldn't publish Rose's work, and I knew I couldn't destroy it. But to do nothing—to let everything gather dust, store her laptop forever in a closet—that would be the most cowardly thing of all, I believed, because it would be destruction without accountability. I kissed her forehead.

Her eyes were already closed. For a while she wore the wig in the house, even though it was only the two of us, but not anymore. Her head was pale. She smelled like a more intense version of herself. I sat beside her and found her hand beneath the sheet and held it while she dozed. I wished for her not to experience any breakthrough pain, while the sun went down and time moved slowly onward toward the next dose.

I had convinced Amanda that we were publishing her daughter's book; the next morning, I set about telling my staff that we were *not* actually publishing the girl's manuscript—just printing a small run of professional-looking copies.

I needn't have worried about their reaction. "Of course," they said. "Let's do this," they said.

Afterward, Paul followed me into my office. "I didn't mean to be cynical yesterday, by the way," he told me. "That was dumb."

I told him not to worry about it.

"Do I look worried?" he said.

We began, at a much-accelerated pace, the many things that went into making a book. The only problem was that I was having a hard time reaching the girl's mother. Within a day I had a mock-up of a cover for them to see. And there were a few editorial questions—some grammatical errors I wanted to correct but didn't want to come off as intrusive. For two days, I left messages. I couldn't help thinking that if the girl were doing well, the mother would have returned my calls. I feared that time was of the essence. And so on Friday evening, I left work early and drove myself to the clean, well-lighted place where I'd become enough of a regular over the summer to garner generous pours. And after enough whiskey to steel myself, I drove to the address printed on the cover page of the girl's manuscript to see if Emma was up to meeting her editor and perhaps conducting a bit of pressing editorial business.

They lived in the Rockland neighborhood, where the city's best homes stood. The CEOs lived here, the CFOs. Not just the lawyers—the partners. The orthopedic surgeons, not the pediatricians. The man who opened the door had on gray slacks and a dress shirt with the sleeves rolled up.

I introduced myself. No recognition from the husband. I mentioned his wife having come to my office.

"Oh, yeah—she mentioned something about a book. Okay. Well, come on in." He led me to their kitchen.

A very domestic scene: family at dinner. Two kids, two parents. Spaghetti on plates. A yellow salad bowl. Seeing me, Amanda looked alarmed.

"I didn't mean to intrude on your dinner," I said. "I called a couple of times." This family was not under duress. I exhaled. My panic had been unfounded. The girl, whom I recognized from the photo as Emma, had a half-eaten plate of pasta in front of her. She looked healthy—not like someone who was being harangued by those who wanted her to drink her Ensures. "I had some editorial questions," I told the mother.

"We should talk in private," she said.

"Wait. Is *he*..." Emma's eyebrows raised. "Oh, man." She shook her head. "Oh, Mom."

I looked to Amanda for clarification. "We're having second thoughts," she said, standing up.

"*Mom.*"

"Like I said, let's you and I go into the other room."

"I'm not dying," Emma said matter-of-factly. "That's what she has to tell you."

I didn't know what to say to that. It was something to celebrate, but no one seemed celebratory.

"Tell him, Mom," she said.

Amanda watched her daughter, then sighed impatiently. "So I might have exaggerated," she told me. "But you have to understand, she wanted a book. She's an excellent poet."

"So . . . she's in remission?" I asked.

"What?" The girl rolled her eyes. "*No*. I'm president of the national honor society and co-captain of the field hockey team. And I volunteer at the animal shelter. And I'm in key club, whatever the hell that is. Same as every other good student." When I didn't reply, she glared at me as if I were dense. "To get into a top college these days, you need something . . . extra."

My whiskey-primed gut began to understand. My brain lagged behind. It was hot in the house. The kitchen fan hummed. "Extra?"

Amanda was now raising her hands in defense.

"My allegiance is to my daughter," she said. "I'm her mother. I have a duty to advocate for her."

"My mom's crazy, by the way," Emma said. "We were only joking about it. I didn't think she'd actually go and *do* it."

"Oh, lord," said her father, who appeared to be a step even behind me.

"My brother's going to have it so much easier," Emma said. "He's an idiot." The brother in question, maybe twelve years old, was stuffing his mouth with spaghetti.

"Just so I'm clear," I said to the girl. "You're healthy?"

"She has psoriasis," her mother said.

The girl groaned. "Yeah, Mom, my elbows itch a lot. Come on, admit it—you lied like a rug."

The boy swallowed. "My sister, the poet," he said.

"I didn't know about any of this," Mr. Sims told me, walking me to my car. Dusk was coming on. Families all across the neighborhood were starting their weekends. It was warm outside but not oppressive like the house had been. A gentle breeze kept the air moving. "That's not a *mea culpa*, by the way. I thought I'd be a more involved parent. But I work seventy hours a week, you know? That kind of life, it isn't compatible with—well, with much. What I'm saying is, I didn't know, but it's my fault, too. There's way too much pressure on these kids."

His speech confirmed that he was an attorney.

"You're full of shit," I informed him.

He stopped walking. "Excuse me?"

I was thinking about every wonderful poet whose manuscript representing years of images and ideas and emotions lay unread in slush piles and in editors' inboxes, never finding the readers they deserved. I was thinking about the hundreds of manuscripts, many of them excellent, that I reject every year. "It's so fucking hard for even a great poet to get her work published," I said.

Mr. Sims took in his immaculate lawn, his immaculate neighborhood. "No," he said. "You know what's hard? Getting into Yale."

I almost laughed and cried at the same moment. Our ambitions were all so stupid and proved nothing. Everything felt absurd and unreal: the fact that it was September already, burned leaves on the ground, each day shorter than the one before. A quarter of a year without Rose. My house was too empty. My evenings were too empty. After Rose died, Paul had encouraged me to take time off. Told me to travel. *What do you know about loss?* I'd thought at the time. He was right, though. I needed to change something big, feel something different.

"Punch me in the face," I told Mr. Sims. He looked like an ex-athlete—thickened from too many meals with clients, but strong.

"Huh?"

"Do it."

He stared at me. "Why would I do that?"

"Just fucking do it." I imagined taking notes and sending them to that professor in Florida, and this, too, almost made me laugh and cry.

"Look, man, you need to drive away," he said.

I shoved him in the chest. It was the first time I'd shoved anybody since I was a kid.

He didn't stumble—good core strength—and to his credit (or, as likely, understanding the moment's potentially litigious nature), he continued not to punch me. Just stared at me with vague curiosity and brushed some fake grit off his shirt. "Go home," he said.

The idea came to me on the drive. I even had a title: *Before Their Time*. Each chapter would profile a poet with talent and promise who died before his or her work made it to book form. I would edit the volume, working with the families of the deceased on the poets' biographies and choosing their best work—maybe a half-dozen poems each. I'd preface the anthology with an essay that directly took on the ethical question of publishing work without the author's consent.

I was so revved up that I called Paul on the drive. "So what do you think?"

"Sure," he said. "I like it."

And because it was Paul, I knew he was telling the truth.

"You all right, Sean?" he asked. "You sound a little off."

"Sure, I'm okay." I decided to wait until Monday to tell him that we wouldn't be printing up the teenager's manuscript after all.

But by the time I was home making dinner in my quiet kitchen, I was already dismissing the idea for the anthology and feeling the lethargy that came from realizing an idea was no good after all.

I didn't care about those poets. Only Rose.

I ate a sandwich and drank a beer and paged through her third and final manuscript. It really was her best work.

Much later, in bed with the lights off, I came up with another idea. Her first two manuscripts I would leave alone. And her newest work, I'd promised never to lay eyes on. But that third manuscript—it deserved readers, deserved to live.

Chad would create a magnificent cover. It wouldn't be sold, this book. It wouldn't even be a book. No sales in stores or online. No barcode. I'd give away copies to friends and family and keep a few around the house.

Some hours later, I awoke to use the bathroom. The idea still seemed good. That's how I knew it was real.

Not a book, I told myself in the bathroom mirror. Not a book.

I could only hope she wouldn't think too poorly of me. But all my other wishes were used up. This was the one I had left.

Quick Change

I

James, I consider you a friend and a worthy companion," Suzanna Mudd told me, an assessment that sounded, coming from her lips, less like praise and more like prelude to an indictment. Long ago, we had played marbles together in the dirt. For years, we walked the last three blocks to school together. In class, I was the only student from whom she deemed worthy of cheating. The feeling was reciprocal. Outside of school we didn't socialize, a fact that accounted for my perfect attendance. I dreaded graduation.

But now it was 1911, and in the two years since we donned and shed our caps and gowns and our peers began to pair, or flee, or care for ailing parents, or as they simply joined the vast dull hum of adulthood, Suzanna and I, to my surprise and delight, found ourselves in continued proximity because of our mutual employment with her father's newspaper. I'd been summoning my courage (finally; glacially) to revealing my feelings toward her—but hearing, now, about my friendliness and companionability, those most cocker spaniel of traits, my body clutched in anticipatory dread. Was she terminally ill? Secretly engaged? I didn't want to hear whatever lay beyond the inevitable conjunction. "But," she said, "I'm afraid you're stunted and egocentric."

I exhaled with relief. Was that all? To my understanding, civilization itself was shaped by the whims of stunted, egocentric men.

We'd been speaking about New York City. She'd never been. Neither had I. We'd never been anywhere, a shared condition we vowed, in time, to remedy, and the recent opening of the New York Public Library provided us with the perfect destination. One million books nestled together; the only image more breathtaking was that of the two of us nestled together for the four-hour train ride.

Her father would never allow it, she told me. Or, worse, he'd insist on coming along, to which I said, "Nonsense—I'll look after you," to which she said the bit about my being a worthy companion, *but*.

"What I'm trying to say," she said, peering at me through eyeglasses that only made her lovely eyes larger, "is I don't believe you'd rush to my defense if I were ever truly threatened."

"Threatened?" I said. "Like by a bear? Because I can't imagine there are many bears in Manhattan."

She shook her head and kept walking. It was a glare-filled June afternoon, like an overexposed photograph, and we were on our way to her father's house—she because she lived there, I to deliver my latest article for edits. The article, about the new beach umbrella rental sheds opening this summer, had proven surprisingly stubborn, probably because it mattered so little. I'd finished in the nick of time, just an hour before the quick-change artist was due to arrive. All week, his piercing black pupils had watched me from the quarter-page advertisements in the *Daily Wave*, our earnest newspaper for which I produced three articles per week in order to afford my horrid apartment over a shop that sold women's undergarments.

Some days, I finished my twelve column-inches in less time than it took to drink my morning coffee. Suzanna knew about this but didn't tell her father, though it was no secret that I considered the *Wave* only after I considered the contents of my cupboard, the dust in the corners of my apartment, and the premature recession of my hairline. But ambition isn't oxygen, everywhere at once. No; it's a sharpshooter's bullet. I refused to tax myself with coming up with new adverbs to describe another nuptial or funeral, but only because I was reserving my passions for what came after my column-inches were done: writing my own fictions, and wooing Suzanna. Regarding the former, I had begun achieving a touch of success publishing locked-room mystery stories and was determined to make a literary career. (My father and mother were pig farmers, a life unsuitable to me due to my severe straw allergies and my genuine admiration for pigs.)

My latter project followed a slower trajectory, beginning with those marble games of yore. Now, both twenty-two, we remained kindred spirits. We were unmarried, restless, and faithful to the notion that we would make our marks and our marks would not be in Cape May, New Jersey.

We walked along now, passing clothiers and the good bakery and the bad bakery, her posture as erect as ever. Her hair—long, wavy, like gentle ripples of sand—had always drawn glances. But her posture, that was the real show, her body elongated and resolute. "Not a bear, James," she said long after I'd assumed we'd moved on. "But you're fundamentally uncourageous. I truly believe that."

How I burned to prove her wrong! I wanted to reach out—right in the middle of the day, right in the middle of Washington Street—take her by the shoulders, and kiss her. The kiss would be imperfect, off-balance and toothy. Afterward, we would stand facing each other, shocked and changed. We would laugh, and maybe cry, because it was a kiss so long overdue.

"I have courage," I told her.

"That's sweet you think so," she said. "But no. The instinct isn't in you."

As the advertisements were quick to boast, the Great Lehigh was not only a preeminent conjurer of mysteries but a world traveler. This was true. There was a time, not so many years ago, when he'd performed for kings and inspired more wonder and gossip across the globe than Houdini (to everyone except Houdini).

Also true, however, was that times change, and since his return to the States, the Great Lehigh had been out of the limelight. But now, after several years, he was back with a new act, testing it in select smaller venues before moving on to performances in Philadelphia and New York and Chicago. Hearing about his upcoming visit from Casey Clark, who managed the Forum Theatre, I'd immediately foreseen three articles: an advance feature, followed, upon the performer's arrival, by an in-depth interview. And after the performance, a review.

I'd hurried straight to Sid Mudd's office and made a case for my own special insight into the quick-change artist's machinations.

"Misdirection," I told him, "and the red herring. These techniques aren't so different from—"

"You're giving me a headache," Mudd said. "I get it. You're a mystery man, he's a mystery man." He knew about my recent short stories. "Fine. It's yours. But demand a full-page ad. Lord knows he can afford it."

Now I stood on the platform beside Casey holding a bow-wrapped box of saltwater taffy while the train (an engine plus three cars) ground to a stop. This was the Great Lehigh's fabled Caravan of Amazement: the first car, for the quick-change artist himself, was modeled after Queen Victoria's saloon carriage, and replete with stateroom, parlor, kitchen, and observation deck. The second car, rumored to be as luxurious as the first, was for his pet Pomeranian. The third car housed the crew, as well as stage sets, costumes—everything needed for the performance. All around us, Cape May was enacting its own gutsy performance. Brine in the air, waves smashing on the beach. Whipping winds shoving layers of gray across the sky. A fierce storm without rain.

A man in a beige coat stepped from the first car onto the platform, carrying a worn black satchel, and I was reminded about the artifice of promotional photos. The real man was less than average height, and with no music to his step, no boldness in his bearing. His moustache, which in his photograph extended perfectly parallel to the ground, drooped like leaves of a forgotten houseplant. I told myself not to be disappointed. We build up the wealthy and successful in our minds.

We approached him, and Casey introduced himself.

"I'm Willard," the man said. Casey and I exchanged a confused glance. A few more men and one woman stepped off the same car carrying their own bags. The crew, I realized, just as the door to the second car opened and a man stepped onto the platform wearing a fur coat and a toothy smile. He came over. I was wrong. The quick-change artist more than did his photo justice, and I felt myself taking a half-step backward as Casey once again introduced himself.

"When can we check out the theater and begin unloading?" asked the Great Lehigh.

"Whenever you like, sir," Casey said. "After supper?"

"Anything wrong with now?"

Casey said now would be fine. I gave him the subtlest of elbows to the kidney. "And this is Mr. Piper," he said.

"From the *Daily Wave*," I said. "Please, call me

James." I handed the quick-change artist the box in my hands. "This is salt-water taffy, made right here in—"

"Sticks to my teeth," he said, and passed the box to the stocky woman. He gazed around, sniffed the air. Clapped his hands once, which got his crew's attention. "Well, let's do this."

As he turned to walk away, I blurted out, "Your publicist said an interview would be—"

He swiveled and peered at me as if I were something washed ashore, a cracked shell or maybe a small dead fish. "Come by my car at ten o'clock."

Ten o'clock was terrible, too late to finish the piece for the morning edition. Besides, Suzanna had made me promise to debrief her about the interview afterwards, and a midnight rendezvous, even having to do with the *Wave*, would never sail with her father.

"Is there any chance—"

"No," he said. "Whatever it is, there's no chance."

A small scar above his left eyebrow gave the man's stare an added edge of intensity.

"Ten is perfect," I said.

"And your dog?" I asked. "Is it true her car is as. . ."—I considered my euphemisms—"*comfortable* as your own?"

"Her car? Do you think I'm crazy, man? Ginger rides with me."

It was quarter past ten, and the Great Lehigh was true to his word. At ten he'd been waiting just outside the second of the train cars. I had anticipated the extravagance of the Queen Victoria's carriage car yet was unprepared for the effect of experiencing it firsthand. Every surface gleamed; anything capable of being carved or molded—table and chair legs, doors, lamps—was done so with intricacy in mind. We sat together on blue velvet chairs, he and I and Suzanna, whom I had invited along, believing she'd find it interesting. Believing, too, she'd be grateful to me for giving her this glimpse into a life of wealth and extravagance.

The dog in question—primped brown fur haloing a graying muzzle—snored atop a nearby velvet loveseat.

"Then what's inside the third car?" Suzanna asked.

"Sets, instruments, everything we need to put on the show," he said, "including. . ." The Great Lehigh lifted the champagne flute to his lips. Our glasses were heavy crystal with swan etchings. I was terrified of setting mine down too hard on its marble coaster. "Well, I shouldn't tell you," he said with a slight smirk. He drank quickly—this was his second glass in only a few minutes, and I wouldn't have bet on his sobriety even when I arrived. "Wouldn't want to spoil the surprise."

He was no actor; clearly, he invited speculation. He wanted to deepen the mystery of himself before I slid a sheet of paper into the typewriter. But speculation took time, and he'd granted me just thirty minutes. I opened my notebook and began to ask him my prepared questions. He wasn't a very good interview, maybe because he'd given too many of them. I continued to endure his prepared, banal answers to my prepared questions, feeling the opportunity for real insight evaporating. Finally, the Great Lehigh saved our interview with a loud, uncovered yawn. It was so disrespectful I wanted to thank him. I shut my interview notebook and, assisted by the glass of wine, asked him what I actually wanted to know.

"When you create your act," I said, "how do you see the whole thing?"

He held his empty glass, eyeing it as if trying to sleuth out where the liquid had gone. "Come again?"

"I want to write mysteries," I said. "I mean, I do write them."

"So you've told me."

It's true. I had told him, shortly upon entering his carriage, in the hope that he might see me as more than just another small-town journalist.

"He's very good," Suzanna added. "I've read them all."

For which I'd thanked her before. I thanked her

again now. "The trouble is, though," I said to the quick-change artist, "I never seem to be able to see around the story to the beautiful reveal."

The wine, plus my confession—never before uttered; not to Suzanna, and barely to myself—made my face heat to an almost unbearable temperature. But it was true. I held deep doubts about my own talent, which maddened me all the more because of all the things I was learning to do. I'd always had a knack for intriguing premises, but I had been studying Henry James for his syntactical playfulness and Charles Dickens for his brilliance with character quirks and demeanor (and names). I had tried penning stories with Poe's brooding moods and Conan Doyle's stodgy narration. By now, I could do many things. All I could not do, in fact, was simply that which a writer of mysteries must: be one step ahead. Be clever. And despite the many admirable qualities of my stories, the result of hours of toiling at my desk reworking sentences until they shined like gems, they weren't clever. I knew this because I was cursed with being just clever enough to know what my stories were: simply, grievously *polished*. There was no magic to them. Nothing ineffable rising above the technique. And while my recent publications should have buttressed me—should have been evidence that I was not toiling in vain—I couldn't help suspecting (no; *knowing*) that my publications resulted not from editors reading my work and falling off their chairs in astonishment, but rather from those same editors being desperate to fill up an issue, editors as hurried and deadline-driven as Sid Mudd, coming across a manuscript that would need only a little copyediting—a manuscript that would, at the very least, make its readers feel clever. Between the acts of finishing my story and mailing my acceptance, I couldn't shake the belief that these editors didn't celebrate. They shrugged.

The Great Lehigh seemed to be deliberating whether to continue his pat answers or indulge me. Finally, he cracked his neck, sat back in his chair, and said, "Are you writing a story now?"

I told him I was.

"Tell me the premise."

I told him. A prisoner is found murdered in his own locked cell.

"Many possibilities there," he said.

"I agree. I've developed several of them. Each is more predictable than the last."

"You're too hard on yourself," Suzanna said, but I felt she'd spoken less to comfort me than to reinsert herself into the conversation.

The Great Lehigh reached into the breast pocket of his blazer and removed a pack of playing cards. He slid the cards from the pack and began to shuffle and cut them elegantly without once looking at his hands.

"The key," he said, "is to start with a breathtaking ending. Begin with that. Then devise your method backwards."

"But I lack the imagination—"

"I'll tell you my secret, if you want. I have only one."

"Please," I said. "Of course."

He set down the pack of cards, learned toward me, and said, "Practice." Sensing my disappointment he quickly added, "You don't understand. You think you do, but you don't. I'm saying practice more than anyone can fathom. More than anyone would believe was possible. You've probably thought of a half-dozen solutions to your prison-cell murder. But a half-dozen won't do. You need to think of fifty. Then winnow it down. Choose the best one and write the ending ten different ways." Now that he was no longer reciting canned responses to familiar questions, he sounded passionate and a little desperate. A bit of spittle collected on his lower lip. "When I change from one costume to another in the blink of an eye, some call it magic. Some call it trickery. Some call it a miracle. They're all wrong, and in the same way. They're looking for the shortcut—the loophole. They could never imagine how much practice went into doing what they just saw!" The Pomeranian's ears twitched. "Practicing moves tens of thousands of times over *years* to shave off tenths of a second. That's my secret. No gimmicks. No trickery. Just work. What I've just said does not go in your paper."

I wanted to believe him because it would mean magnificence was under my control. But I feared he was like a gull explaining flight to a heavy-boned, wingless creature.

The quick-change artist wasn't done. "And what I've given up," he said, taking another drink. "No one considers that, either. Whom I've shunned, what I've missed in the service of total commitment. I once had family and friends. Now I have staff. True professionals, keepers of secrets . . . but it's not the same. I pay them well for their loyalty."

"You've traveled the world," Suzanna said. "You've met King George."

"It's true, young lady. I've been party to pomp, to spectacle. But I'll tell you something. I have seen the world, and the world is fickle. It loves you one day, and the next day it decides it prefers a half-size Hungarian huckster with flexible joints." He chased his words with the last of his wine. "This is real. Sitting here with you both." He picked up the bottle and looked at it with disapproval, and then to me. "This damn bottle is empty, and you're a damn struggling artist, and you"—turning to Suzanna—"are simply damn delightful—but not simple, this I would bet my life on." He walked to a tall cabinet with the slight sway of a man riding the rails, except the car wasn't moving. In the cabinet were various liquors, and he returned with three fresh tumblers and a bottle of Scotch. He opened the bottle and poured.

"Now," he said to me, glass raised, "tell me more about your prison-cell story. I'll wager the solution is already within your grasp."

I told him. And while he shuffled his cards, he spoke about lightness and darkness, about expectation and its denial. Above all, he spoke about wonderment. I jotted notes so I'd forget nothing. Suzanna tucked a whisp of hair behind her ear, her telltale sign of deep concentration, and got into the act: not perfunctorily. Not to remind us of her presence. She was part of this, and I felt proud of her, proud to have invited her tonight, and we all laughed at something the Great Lehigh said, and I imagined our laughter carrying outward past the train car, the station, carrying on the wind all the way down the beach, and when the bottle was empty, our conversation was not, and we stayed at it, talking and tinkering, inching our way toward some breathtaking leap of the imagination, and then the Great Lehigh swallowed more Scotch and let it slip that it was a wild animal in the second car, a five-hundred-pound beast, part of a new routine, possibly his greatest ever, and he would tell us more except he wanted us to experience it fully. It was becoming exactly the evening I'd hoped for when I imagined getting to spend time with this most accomplished of performers, and I kept reminding myself of this, and gradually I was able to stop stealing glances at Suzanna, whose rapt expression had not once, in all these years, been gifted to me.

We shuffled along the quiet dirt road, Suzanna and I, toward our side of town. It was late—well past midnight. I imagined the bustle of New York City at this time of night. There, we would just be getting started.

She stopped. "Oh, shoot."

"What is it?"

"I was supposed to get him to agree to an ad. My father . . . that's why he let me come."

"I'm sure tomorrow—"

"No, he was quite clear about it."

We'd been walking only a couple of minutes. I turned around. "Then let's head back."

She started back with me a few steps, then stopped again. "You know what?" she said. "You go on home. I don't mind going alone."

The only light came from the moon. The only sounds were crickets and the wind blowing through a grove of scraggly trees. "Didn't I promise to look after you?" I said.

"I can look out for myself." She sounded more stern than the moment warranted. Then her voice softened. "Really. You go home."

I watched her in the moonlight and my world tilted. "Are you sure?" My voice sounded as needling as sawgrass.

She reached out and touched my arm. "Good night, James." She began walking back to the station.

We went in opposite directions. When she was out of sight, I retraced my steps to where we'd parted ways and sat in the dirt. I clenched and unclenched my fists and listened to the crickets.

She was right, of course. I was not courageous. Not ever. I lacked the very instinct that bears and wolves and sharks and all the world's brutes possessed in abundance. But instinct becomes unnecessary in the face of planning, I told myself, and decided to believe it.

I stood, brushed off my pants, and started home. One day wasn't nearly enough time to develop an ironclad alibi for what I had to do. But a day was all I had. The Great Lehigh had only the one show before moving on to Philadelphia and then New York. And I knew, as much as I ever knew anything in this sluggish seaweed of a town, that if I failed to act, when the train pulled out Suzanna would be on it.

II

Who among us reveals everything? Even an adequate journalist prepares adequately, and during such preparation I came across a review of the Great Lehigh's prior performance in Harrisburg, PA. From that article, I was nearly certain that the quick-change artist's Caravan of Amazement would be carrying the most unusual of feline cargo. Hearing it confirmed by the man himself meant I now knew the basic narrative of his finale, which a gushing Raymond Van de Sande of the *Harrisburg Gazette* had called "the most heart-stopping performance this theater-goer has ever witnessed."

The effect was thus: The quick-change artist, dressed in rags, is caught stealing a pie cooling on a windowsill. Two policemen (his assistants) handcuff him and wrap him in metal chains. The assistants then leave the stage and return wheeling a steel-barred cage containing an all-too-real tiger. The animal paces. It roars. The policemen lead the shackled, trembling quick-change artist toward the cage and shove him inside. They throw a curtain over the cage. Seconds later, a scream, presumably the pie-thief meeting his demise—but no!—for the tiger suddenly bursts forth from beneath the curtain, having escaped its cage, and is about to leap into the terrified audience, when the animal's head *lifts off* to reveal the quick-change artist inside what is now—somehow, impossibly—a convincing tiger costume. The guards/assistants remove the curtain from the steel cage. The quick-change artist's chains and handcuffs lie on the floor of the cage. The real tiger has vanished. The quick-change artist takes a much-deserved bow.

Reading the article prior to the Great Lehigh's arrival, I marveled at the effect while pondering its method. Now, while Cape May slept, I burned a candle and sat at my small table considering it again. I knew the ending of the routine; therefore, I knew the ending of the quick-change artist's life. I'd known it the moment Suzanna said, "Good night, James." I suppose that was one reason why I'd wept.

When I was a boy, my father would take me hunting, which I did not enjoy. He taught me to shoot and was confounded by my ineptitude, unaware that I was learning accuracy by carefully avoiding hitting the deer that munched innocently on wild blackberries and rosebud leaves.

My father soon returned to hunting alone, though when I moved from the farm to town, he gifted me a Colt Model 1903 pocket hammerless handgun. *A man needs to be able to protect what's his*, he told me. I had never fired it, nor had I planned to, and relegated the gun to a drawer full of half-forgotten objects of nostalgia: a smooth piece of driftwood; a yellowed Buster Brown comic; the award I'd received for writing the best essay about President Roosevelt.

Tomorrow, the Great Lehigh would spring himself from the tiger's cage in a costume that had made Harrisburg leap in fright. In roughly twenty hours, I would be seated close to the stage beside the woman I loved. When the finale arrived, I would be the hero. The tiger would escape its cage, and I would save Suzanna (and the whole audience, besides) by shooting dead the convincingly real animal before it could attack.

I knew the authorities wouldn't question my carrying of the handgun. Among the men in town, a firearm by one's side was nothing out of the ordinary. The Great Lehigh's murder would be viewed—by the authorities, by the world—as a regrettable misunderstanding. For a while, I would be a subject of the press. I would effuse horror and sorrow. Some would damn me, though even in the damning there would be an air of respect, for I had acted to save my fellow theatergoers.

Suzanna would be in shock at first. Then she would see what I had done for her, the courage I indeed possessed.

He would do anything for me, she would realize.

I would. I would. I would.

Thus motivated, I planned every action and considered every variable long after the first roosters called and the sky began to brighten and my eyes became tired and raw. Still, there were questions I couldn't answer, questions that kept me from resting my head: When the moment came, would I truly take aim and pull the trigger? If I pulled the trigger, would the gun (cleaned and oiled, but never used) fire, or would it jam?

I reflected back to our time in the train car—the interview-turned-artists' salon, those two glorious hours before everything had become grotesque—and I wondered, was there even a real tiger on that stage in Harrisburg, and on the train now, or only a convincing costume and a rumor slyly spread by the quick-change artist himself? I tried, for the first time, to entertain the logistics of traveling with an animal of such size and ferocity—the danger, the pounds of raw meat, the mucking of its cage without the mucker becoming supper—and thought: there was no way. This was not a traveling circus. The Great Lehigh would need a larger crew. And who would go through so much trouble and expense for a single routine lasting perhaps four minutes?

Of course, I knew exactly who would. And if, by the time his train wheeled into town that week in June, 1911, the quick-change artist's star was already fading, then all the more reason for him to persist with the extravagance his persona demanded.

As for the quality of his performance on stage some twelve hours later, I'll say this: until the moment I pulled the trigger, the Great Lehigh more than met his moniker.

The evening began with Casey Clark welcoming everyone to his humble theater, then introducing the evening's performer with an unctuous bow. Then: music! His assistants, between deftly preparing sets and setting props, took turns accompanying the quick-change artist's routines with exotic melodies, further casting a spell on the audience—violin and cello; then a guitar and a sort of large flute I'd never before seen; then they clapped and stomped syncopated percussion.

Suzanna and I watched, side by side, gaping at these routines performed for kings. We gasped and applauded along with three hundred other theatergoers, and as each minute passed, I came to understand that the performer on stage was a liar. Practice, he had told me in presumed confidence. Practice. Had he and Suzanna laughed at me afterwards, back in his quarters? Because the true, disappointing secret being revealed to me now was that no accumulation of minutes and hours, alone, could ever result in the spectacle before my eyes. Practice alone did not account for the ineffable, for God or lightning or the luck of genius. Not every dedicated telegraph operator invents the lightbulb. There was diligence, and then there was *this*, and I knew—watching costumes melt into other costumes before my unblinking eyes, while the man on-stage moved with ballet-like fluidity—that I was a fool for briefly believing otherwise.

I would not become a great author. My stories might entertain but would never amaze. Knowing this, I felt a great burden lift as I settled into my seat and let myself enjoy the show. Beneath my jacket, my gun. Seated to my left, a transfixed, dressed-to-the-nines beauty who every so often would clutch my forearm without knowing it. Each time, my heart sped up, though it would not begin to race in earnest until the lights went dark, as stage sets were reconfigured yet again, then came back on to reveal the façade of a storefront. A windowsill. A pie.

The routine proceeded according to the description in the *Harrisburg Gazette*. To a somber string accompaniment, the quick-change artist enters from stage left dressed in baggy trousers and a shabby overcoat. He spots the pie and dares to creep closer. A glance to the left, right. Silently, he lifts the pie and tiptoes back from whence he came, when: a police whistle! The thief freezes. A second policeman enters from stage right. The first officer grasps the thief's shoulders to keep him in place while the second snaps on handcuffs. The second officer holds up a finger—aha; an idea—and marches offstage, returning a moment later carrying heavy chains. They shackle the thief, then frown, dissatisfied. The second officer holds up his finger again. He motions for the two musicians to follow him off-stage. Moments later, they return wheeling a large cage.

The audience gasped. So did I. How could one not? This was no costume. Inside the cage, the tiger—immense and absolutely real—paced, tail swishing. As if on cue, when the two policemen urged the thief toward the cage, the tiger emitted a deadly, hungry roar, eliciting screams from more than a few in the audience. I'd read somewhere that a tiger's roar carries several miles in the wild. I believed it.

We were seated in the fifth row, center. Suzanna clutched my left arm with both hands.

"The man is insane," I whispered as the Great Lehigh approached the iron cage. Surely, the tiger would tear him apart. I couldn't imagine my gun would be needed. One last frightened look from the thief (which would have come across as melodramatic had the tiger not been genuine), and the two policemen took hold of the iron door and slid it open just enough to shove the Great Lehigh inside before slamming it shut again.

After that, everything happened fast. The two musicians, whom I hadn't noticed had left the stage, returned with a red curtain, which they draped over the top of the cage. It billowed and settled. Then the chilling, sustained scream. Policeman Number One peeked behind the curtain and—acting shocked—recoiled and yanked away the curtain.

The door sprung open; the animal emerged. My god, it looked real, a sartorial marvel. Had I not been forewarned, I would have believed it to be the same animal. But having been forewarned, and thus being somewhat inured, I could see that it was not. The girth, the stance, the quality of the fur, the way the head connected to the neck. The subtlest variations, nothing to notice, unless you knew the truth.

I raised my gun. More screams from the audience as the animal reared up by the edge of the stage. I took aim and fired. My father taught me well.

When the Great Lehigh fell to the stage floor, the assistants were of course the first to know that something had gone wrong. They approached him, unsure what had just happened, but unwilling, for the moment, to act—knowing that to intervene would be to break the audience's spell. Then the woman assistant who had played such sweet notes on the violin all night long cried out, "We need a doctor!" and the house lights came on, and the ushers began quickly to escort everyone from the theater.

"James," Suzanna was saying. "James. James." She seemed unable to go beyond that. I led her toward the aisle, placing an arm around her warm waist to guide her away from the stage. We were caught up in the current of theatergoers, though I did turn my head to glimpse what I had caused. The staff had gathered. The costume's head had been removed, and I caught a peek of the thick dark hair of the Great Lehigh, prostrate in his tiger costume, which, now that it was motionless, did not look so real after all. The violinist wailed.

The identity of the shooter didn't become known right away. Only a few people had seen me raise the gun, and afterward there was a general ruckus. In the hours that followed, several Jameses better known in town than I became the man who shot the tiger, which, people began to understand, was not a tiger at all. In the end, Suzanna's father was responsible for clearing up the confusion, penning a brief column for the morning paper. In addition to naming the correct James, he set the restrained tone for the articles to follow in other papers over the coming days. The common theme: a tragic misunderstanding that stood as testament to the genius of the deceased performer. The policeman who questioned me was unceasingly polite and appeared concerned mostly about the trauma I had suffered and the guilt I would bear.

For a couple of days, I kept to myself as I came to terms with what I had done. My mother visited with meals. I waited for Suzanna, and when she didn't come, I went to her father's house. When I entered, she was seated at the table. She had clearly been crying. When I sat down beside her, she moved her chair away. She and I had little time to speak after the events themselves—right after we left the theater, her father (who'd been sitting in the balcony and hadn't yet known I was the shooter) had thanked me for leading his daughter to safety, shaken my hand, and taken her home.

He told us now what he'd just learned—that the quick-change artist's funeral would be held the following Saturday morning at Glover's Church.

"Here?" I asked.

Several apples lay on the countertop, and Mr. Mudd began touching one, then another. "It seems he didn't have family or an attachment to any particular place. An assistant who handled his personal affairs claims this was as good a place as any."

"But . . ." I was about to say, *He performed for Kings!* I tried to be more precise. "Shouldn't his funeral be more commensurate with his stature?"

Mr. Mudd had selected an apple and taken a bite. He chewed in thought. "I'm guessing he cares less about that now."

The next day, I returned with cookies from the good bakery. I sat beside Suzanna and watched her nibble in thought or memory or idleness. Her eyes were dry, and she seemed distracted. I asked if she planned to attend the funeral. She nodded.

"Would you care to go together?"

Another nod.

"It isn't the New York Public Library, I'm afraid."

The corners of her mouth lifted slightly into what might generously be called a smile. She looked beautiful in the morning light streaming through the window, and I came as close as I'd ever come to telling her that I loved her and always had and always would. But even I knew my timing for such a declaration could be better chosen.

Patience, I reminded myself, for time was no longer my enemy.

Saturday morning was sunny and cool. I tapped on the Mudds' front door and waited. I tapped again, waited longer, and decided Suzanna must have accompanied her father. I walked to the church alone, and when I entered I was struck by the oddest sense of familiarity and disorientation: same performer, same audience, only in a new venue. Instead of theatrical lighting, sunlight through stained glass. Instead of seats, pews. Instead of a stage, an altar.

As I scanned for Suzanna, I noticed some in the crowd noticing me because I was momentarily newsworthy. Mr. Mudd was seated beside Casey Clark and his wife, Laura. In the front pew sat some of the quick-change artist's staff. One of them, a woman wearing a simple black dress, sat weeping. I recognized her as the violinist from the performance.

The casket was noticeably plain. It occurred to me I'd been expecting something as ornate as the table legs in the Queen Victoria's carriage, until I recalled the words of my employer: *I'm guessing he cares less about that now*. I approached it for the same reason anyone does: for closure, for one last moment, for irrefutable proof that the end does come for us all.

I found it immeasurably sad that the Great Lehigh would be buried here, in an unfamiliar town of strangers. I wished there had been someone better to curate his eternity. This was my thought as I prepared to face the quick-change artist for the last time.

The undertaker had dressed him in a tasteful gray suit. And as with other funerals I had attended, I primed myself for an uncanny visage that appeared neither alive nor dead nor sleeping. There was a separate state, it seemed, for the embalmed. I knew this as I glanced at the man who had entered and altered my life just days earlier.

I gazed at him, then spun around, or rather the church spun around me, and my eyes locked on the violinist seated just a few feet away. Her stare of pure hatred nearly made my knees buckle.

Somehow, my legs continued providing support as I bolted from the church. In the casket, he had looked wilted. His hair, his mustache. There was no scar above the eyebrow. He looked somewhat like the quick-change artist but more like who he was: the man who'd first stepped off the train, the man I'd briefly mistaken for the Great Lehigh.

I reached the theater. (I must have run the whole way; I remember nothing of the journey but arrived out of breath.) The theater had been shut since last week's performance, the doors locked, but a side window slid open. The theater was silent and lit by just a couple of bulbs. I didn't know how to turn more lights on, so I walked up the left side of the dim theater and climbed onto the empty stage. I could see spike marks on the stage floor for The Great Lehigh and his staff. I didn't know what I was looking for. Something real. Something that made a lick of sense. I saw a half-hearted attempt to clean a man's blood, which had seeped into the stage floor. A few feet behind the stain were the spike marks for the large cage, and within its perimeter, a rectangular marking. No: not a marking. Cuts in the wood. I knelt down, found a small gouge in the floor that fit my fingers, and pulled. Up slid a hinged portion of the stage floor. A trap door. I lay down and peered inside. Nothing but darkness.

I imagined the tiger being lowered below-stage under cover of curtain while the quick-change artist hid behind a mirror at the back of the cage. More likely it was the other way: the tiger was prodded behind the mirrored divider in the cage as the quick-change artist dropped below-stage and out of sight. His double, the man I killed, must have already been below stage, dressed in the tiger costume. When the curtain covered the cage, the divider came down in front of the tiger and the two men changed places. The Great Lehigh had lied: practice alone had not accounted for his miracles. At least not for his newest, greatest effect. There was also, crucially, a convincing double—a double whose performance would now continue on into the infinite.

I thought back to the church, to the grieving violinist, and I wept for her loss. Then I wept for my own. I don't know how long I sat there, but the train's whistle, audible even inside the theater, suggested to me that the funeral had ended.

In the coming days, we would learn that the Great Lehigh's impending tour had been on the brink of disaster. Ticket sales were weak. Creditors were at his door. At the time he'd rolled into the Cape May station, his New York shows had already been canceled. It seemed the city was now enamored with film and a kind of serious art and theater that probed the depths of our unconscious desires, more so than with an aging man's stretched-out vaudeville act.

We were changing, all of us, and it wasn't lost on me, even as I sat on the stage of the Forum Theatre, that I finally had a story worth telling, a story I could tell nobody. I imaged three cars pulling away from the station, and with them all the sets, the costumes, a tiger, a well-compensated staff lighter by one, a pampered Pomeranian, a man named Lehigh, and a woman named Suzanna. The staff, I assumed, would disembark in Philadelphia or maybe New York, where there was more than enough good-paying work for talented stage hands. The latter two, I assumed, would abandon the train sooner in some smaller station. They would opt for simpler modes of transport as they explored their freedom together, heading for destinations I could not fathom, failure to fathom being my fate.

HERO

We had driven halfway across the playa, Tarp and I, one morning when we came across a woman walking our way on the other side of the road.

"Now there's something you don't see every day," Tarp said from the passenger seat.

At 8 a.m. the playa was not yet 50 degrees. My first thought—hell, there was no first thought. It was June. Just a few weeks earlier, the mountains on the California side blazed with yellow and purple flowers and smelled like mint. Now everything was brown and dead. A dozen miles across the salt flats rose the faceless grassy mountains of Nevada. Between the two ranges, the last inch of water had finally evaporated, turning the ten-thousand acres of mud into a brick-hard crust.

My car was the only vehicle on the long, straight road. Whenever I drove across the playa, I imagined breaking down. Even fully clothed, it was no place to get stuck. Not without plenty of water, sunscreen, and time.

I slowed down and cranked the window open. The car was prehistoric. Built into the console was a cassette player that didn't work and a cigarette lighter than did.

Seeing us, the woman on the side of the road stopped, and I called across the road, "You cold?"

She stood hands on hips, waiting, like she was doing us a courtesy. She was maybe sixty. She had on brown sweat socks and nothing else.

"Yeah. Course." Her voice was gruff and fatalistic, like she'd been dealt another losing hand at one of the cheap-ass casinos on the Nevada side.

"You need a ride?"

Her reply was a change in location. For a substantial woman, she moved quickly, leaving me no time even to drape a towel over the backseat. Not that I had a towel. But to hell with my car. I'd bought it thinking a cheap Volvo must be a steal. And it was: I'd been stolen from. Everything was always breaking—engine, electrical, you name it. More than once, Tarp suggested we drive my car into the foothills for target practice, but I believed in doing no violence to flesh or aluminum.

"You going to Canton Mills?" I asked.

"Another guy drove me a few miles," she said. "He kept lecturing me. 'Shouldn't be out here like that.' I told him to go to hell, and I got out."

"Yeah, but where are you headed?"

"I'm headed the way I'm going," she said.

"To Canton Mills." Had to be. The nearest town after that was another thirty miles. The one after that another forty.

Tarp and I, we played those other towns every blue moon. We were a band. Guitar and drums. We didn't have a name, and we only had the two instruments, but that was enough to meet Maria, who'd been sitting at the bar one night, studying, while we were setting up our gear.

"I already walked twenty miles," the woman said.

She was currently or recently kite-high, but her face in the rearview looked determined. You'd have to be determined to cross the salt flats naked. If she'd been walking even half the distance she said, it meant she must have started before sunup. Now the temperature was climbing fast. Another hour under that sun and she'd have gone from hypothermia to heat stroke and massive sunburn. Dying out here took no skill or creativity. My old man taught me that after we came here from Michigan. He put up fences. The outdoor season was longer here, was his thinking. More work days per year. Now that he was gone, I repaired the fences he once built, and I made first-rate cheese grits at the café.

"I'm taking you to Canton Mills," I said, making a U-turn.

"Isn't any of *his* business if I'm naked," she grumbled.

"No, ma'am, it sure isn't," Tarp said.

She'd probably driven into the mountains to get high last night. Watch the stars or whatever. I think there might have been a meteor shower. Maybe her vehicle broke down, or maybe she forgot she ever had one. We weren't so far from Black Rock City, where they hold Burning Man. Wrong time of year, but the ethos stuck around.

When the woman started coughing, I opened the windows, thinking the fresh air might keep her from getting sick in my car.

"You still cold?" Tarp asked.

"Yeah," she said in a fast, serious exhale, and I stepped harder on the gas.

Tarp cranked the heat, and I knew right away that was a bad idea.

The woman said, "And now I'm gonna throw up."

"Not in my Volvo!" I stomped the brake and reached over the seat to get her door open. She got out just in time.

While we waited, Tarp said, "Guess you won't be going to Nevada this morning after all."

"Guess not," I said.

"Well, isn't this mighty convenient?"

I looked over at him. "You think I planned it?"

"Didn't say that. I only said it was convenient."

The first time I was about to break up with Maria, I got called into the café last-minute. Saturday mornings were our busiest time, and we didn't have a deep bench of short-order cooks. The second time, Maria had just received terrible news. It was her score on the LSAT. She was desperate to become a lawyer and help the undocumented people at the Southern border navigate the depravity being forced on them by our elected leaders. This was her second time taking the test, and she'd bombed it worse than the first time. For weeks, anytime she wasn't answering the phones for her stepfather's insurance agency, she parked herself in the library with those test prep books and a stack of 3x5 index cards, but all she seemed to learn was that the shit we want and the shit we're any good at were like two mountain ranges separated by an endless playa.

The past few days, I'd made myself hard to reach. I was laying the groundwork. *Real busy with fences*, I'd texted.

The woman in my car eased herself back and cleared her throat.

"You feeling better now?" I asked.

The heat was off. Windows wide open. My car, my rules.

"Yeah," she said.

"Hey, what's your name?" Tarp asked.

She took a moment remembering or making something up. "Bess."

"I'm Tarp," he said. "He's Chip. We're like your knights in shining armor, aren't we?"

She didn't have anything to say to that other than clearing her throat several times.

I asked, "You gonna be okay if I start driving again?"

"Just don't start lecturing me," she said. "That other guy, he kept lecturing me. Isn't any of his damn business what I do."

"Okay," I said. "But if you feel sick again, give me plenty of warning."

"This piece-of-shit car is Chip's pride and joy," Tarp said once we got moving. "Chip is never gonna part with it."

"One day I will," I said.

"Chip can't part with anything," he went on. "This girl he's seeing—"

"Shut the fuck up," I said, and Tarp laughed.

That's why we'd been crossing the playa. So I could tell Maria, face to face, that our being together was a wrong thing. It needed to happen. There were small things, like the fact that I smoked, or how whenever she laughed, which wasn't often, she looked guilty afterwards. And there were bigger things, like her desperation to move away from all this nothing and, her words, *start her life*. But I didn't mind it here. The way I saw it, there was no bigger threat to the world than an ambitious man, and I was doing my small part to remedy that.

After two failed attempts to cut Maria loose, Tarp didn't trust me to go through with it alone. But now I had this other thing to do, and it wasn't unpleasant to know that the next fifteen minutes would be filled with purpose. Follow the road back to town, deliver this woman to safety. She'd been in real danger from the elements, despite being too high to know it.

"You know anyone in Canton Mills?" I asked the woman, Bess. When she didn't answer, I looked in the rearview. Her head tilted to the side. Fast asleep.

"Let me guess," Tarp said. "You're gonna wait for some other day to break up with Maria. Maybe next never?"

"What do you care? This came up."

"Wasn't this, it'd be something else."

Tarp was recently done with the marriage that had started when he was barely out of high school. Now he was like the guy who discovers a new hot sauce and wants everyone to try it.

"Just text her, for Christ's sake," he said. "That's how everyone breaks up now."

"Nah, I have to do it right," I explained. "Maria deserves that, at least."

"Bullshit. She's irresponsible."

This again? "It's not her fault your damn snare drum got stolen."

Then Tarp reminded me that she'd promised to watch his gear while I was getting our car and he went off to piss, and I reminded him that she was only away from his drums for a minute to get a Sprite from the bar.

The theft put our band on hiatus. With only two instruments, you really need them both.

"She still feels bad about it," I told him.

"Not bad enough to buy me a new snare drum."

"She would if she could afford it," I said. "Man, we've been through this."

Bess snored the last few miles to Canton Mills. In the medical clinic parking lot, I left the engine running and went inside. Gave the woman at the counter a quick rundown of events.

"Well, that's a new one," she said. Which I was sort of glad to hear. She was about forty, and if she'd worked in this clinic a long time, she must have seen just about everything. But apparently not this. "Did she happen to say what happened?"

I looked for a nametag but didn't see one. For a woman who worked the front desk of a run-down clinic, she had an unguarded, interested face. Like an aunt you could confide in, knowing she wouldn't shatter hearing the truth. I took her question to be sincere, not some sly way of asking if maybe I was the cause of Bess's current condition. I didn't look especially upstanding at the moment—you don't dress fancy to break up with your girlfriend—but the clinic was cheap wood-panel walls and stained carpeting and didn't strike me as a place for bullshit and nicety.

"Nah, she didn't say," I told the woman. "Just that

her car broke down. Do you maybe have a blanket or sheet or something you could come outside with?"

She told me to hang on, and went down the hallway and into a room. When I went outside again, Bess was awake and had left the car. Left the parking lot, too, and was standing in the middle of the road. A car honked. So did another.

Tarp was in the parking lot leaning against my car.

"Why'd you let her out?" I asked.

"What was I gonna do?"

"Hey!" I called after her. "Bess! You should come back here."

Nobody was coming out of the clinic, and now the woman was half a block gone. So I called 911 and gave the dispatcher the same rundown I'd given the woman in the clinic. *Older woman, naked in the playa, high or coming down.* I told the dispatcher I'd driven her to the clinic in Canton Mills but she wouldn't go in. "She's walking in the middle of the road," I said.

The dispatcher said, "Can you describe her?"

I thought I already had. "She's wearing brown socks," I said.

Bess had stopped walking and stood in the middle of the street looking straight up at the sky while cars curved slowly around her. Finally, the woman from behind the counter came out of the clinic carrying a folded-up sheet. On her heels came another woman and a man, both in medical scrubs. "Hang on a sec," I told the dispatcher while the first woman trotted over to Bess, who shook her head and kept looking up at the morning sky. There was nothing to see. It was the high desert, and the sky was exactly blue and nothing else. Then they seemed to have a short conversation, which ended with Bess letting the woman wrap the sheet around her. "I think we might be okay," I said to the dispatcher. "I think we've got this under control."

The dispatcher seemed fine with that.

The four of them walked right past me and went

inside. I stood on the sidewalk at the edge of the clinic parking lot and looked around at the ordinary street. Some cars went past. A few pedestrians stood on the sidewalk, one of them bent over a newspaper vending machine. This was as busy as Canton Mills ever got. Tarp was still leaning against my car, looking down at his phone again, seeing if anything anywhere was any different from the last time he checked.

"I can't believe they didn't want our names," I said.

"Who?"

"The clinic people."

"Why would they want that?" he said without looking up from his phone.

I wasn't sure exactly. But letting us leave without getting our names felt incomplete.

I went back into the clinic. The woman at the counter seemed surprised to see me again.

"I thought you might want our names or something," I told her.

She said, "I mean, sure, you can leave them," and handed me a sheet of paper and a pen. While I wrote, she said, "Want to guess why she was standing in the road?"

"Why's that?"

"She said she was stargazing."

"Ha," I said, because we'd been through something together and I could tell she wanted me to have this with her, this small shared laugh. Though it wasn't as if the stars vamoosed in the daytime, and I always kind of liked knowing that just behind all that blue shone every fireball in the heavens.

I added Tarp's name and phone number to the sheet of paper. "I'm Chip," I said. "You can call if you need anything. I've always got my phone with me." It was true. My old man's fences held up remarkably well, but when there's a problem and your animals are getting loose, it's always an emergency.

"Well, thank you, Chip, for doing what you did. It

was very kind of you," the woman said, and smiled, and I knew no one was going to call. After Bess sobered up, she'd have a place to go or she wouldn't. Either way, my part in this was over. Nobody would want anything from us. I thought about Maria, wanting so badly to help strangers in need that she'd move anywhere and go into debt if only some crappy law school would let her in.

"No it wasn't," I said.

"Excuse me?"

I looked at the woman. "What exactly was kind about it? Not leaving her for dead? Not assaulting her?"

"What? *No*. Why would you. . ."

Driving to the clinic, Tarp had told Bess we were her knights in shining armor. I'd felt it, too. A couple of heroes. Which meant my view of myself was no better than this woman's.

"You're thanking me for literally the lowest standard you can hold a person to," I said.

Her body stiffened. Her smile was gone. She didn't like me any longer. "Not everyone would have done it, is all."

"Yeah. Well. Take it up with them."

"You're gonna have to get your car detailed," Tarp said as we pulled out of the clinic lot.

"I don't want to talk about it." Thirty minutes earlier, the day had felt electric and full of purpose, but now all that was gone.

"You couldn't pay me a million bucks to sit back there," Tarp said.

At which point I kicked Tarp out of my car. We weren't more than a mile from his apartment. He'd survive.

I lit a cigarette, and headed solo to Nevada. The real trouble with Maria wasn't her laugh or my smoking or any of that. It was that I believed in her. That was the heart of it. Through sheer force of will, she was going to become a lawyer. Maybe not soon, but eventually. And where would that leave me? I'd never been a big disappointment to anyone and wasn't about to start now.

On the drive, in the middle of the playa, about where we'd stopped for Bess, I pulled my car to the side of the road and stepped into the beaming sun. Nothing but rock-hard crust stretched for miles. Now that she was out of my car, I couldn't help admiring the woman. I tried to imagine what it would feel like to bare myself and just go—to say to myself, fuck the odds—and it occurred to me there was only one way to know.

I drove the rest of the way across the playa and stopped at the CVS for more cigarettes before heading to Maria's apartment. I hadn't called first, and Maria answered her door in sweatpants and an oversized flannel shirt.

"I know for a fact," I told her, offering the packet of index cards I'd bought along with the cigarettes, "the third time is the damn charm."

She stood in the doorway looking bedraggled and resigned and absurdly pretty. "I wouldn't be so sure," she said.

I shrugged. "Me being sure has nothing to do with it. A fact's a fact."

She didn't smile. Didn't say another word. But she took the packet of index cards from me. I followed her inside and shut the door.

America, Etc.

My dad, the drone pilot, is losing to me again at Missile Command. He's only on level three and is already desperate with the joystick, jerking it around and repeatedly stabbing the fire button like it's Morse Code for *I'll be dead in three seconds.* "The smart bombs are too smart!" he says, and winks. But the game we're playing is thirty years old, and trust me, the bombs aren't that smart. And anyway, why is he winking? Maybe if he kept both eyes open, he'd successfully defend more cities.

Mom's in bed. The baby's in her crib being quiet for now. I should probably be in bed, too, since I have basketball in the morning, but while I was brushing my teeth, Dad found me in the bathroom and asked how my thumbs were feeling.

"They're feeling restless," I said.

"Then let's have at it," he said.

That's our routine. So I spat into the sink and followed him downstairs.

"Hands down, this is the best part of my day," he said as the cartridge loaded up and he went to work on the stack of Keebler cookies on the coffee table in front of us.

I shut off the halogen light to make the game look better, and when I returned to the couch, half the cookies were gone. Good thing I'd eaten a few after supper—Dad eats cookies like a Hoover. Especially after a rough day at the office. That's what he calls it. *I'm off to the office; I'm home from the office*—a joke, because he's a pilot, not an accountant. But it's also true that he works in an office. I've seen it from the outside, and it looks like every other brown building on the base. You'd never guess that pilots are in there making actual planes rise and turn and bomb targets halfway around the world. *Your father has a stressful job*, Mom tells me sometimes when Dad complains about having "a rough day at the office" or when he acts sad or too happy for no reason. *Duh*, I always feel like saying to her. *Like, duh*—though before tonight, Dad would never tell me what exactly made the rough days rough. Not that it ever stopped me from asking. But whenever I did, his answer was always a glance over at Mom, who'd intercept: *Jeremy, your father deserves some peace at home.*

Mom is pretty much our translator, especially at the table. Dad talks, Mom translates, I pipe in, Mom translates some more, until eventually I'm excused to the living room to play Nintendo DS. We've got supper conversation pretty much down to a system, mostly thanks to Mom—not surprising, considering that she's an actual translator. Her specialty is Italian novels being published in America, but I think she probably works harder at the kitchen table with us.

So I was kind of shocked when tonight Dad looked right at me over our plates of food and said, "We hit a dog."

"*Reid.*" My mother shot my father a glance—his response was a shrug—and then she got up to refill water glasses.

"Oh," I said. "Huh?"

"One of our Hellfire missiles was about to hit its target when a dog came around the corner."

"Oh." I felt like I ought to say more, now that we had this open channel of communication. Maybe I should console him. But how? And also—why? Because when you're fighting in an actual war like he is against terrorists who would kill every last one of us if they had the chance—even me, even Avery—a dead dog might be sad, but it isn't tragic. It just isn't. "What kind of dog was it?" I asked.

My father looked at me long enough to make it clear I'd messed up somehow, and our open channel closed again. "The kind that barks, Jeremy."

I ate a few more sweet potato fries, nodding and pretending that I hadn't just been shamed.

"Can I be excused now?" I asked.

Yes, I could.

Me, the brown loveseat, my Nintendo DS, and four Keebler chocolate chip cookies stacked on a napkin. That's pretty much bliss, and I get to do it every single night. We live in a house. When I was younger, we lived in an apartment on the base, where Dad worked as a historian. That was his major in college—history. Mom's, too. That was how they met and fell in love. When Mom got pregnant with Avery, Dad changed jobs within the Air Force and trained to become a pilot for remotely powered aircraft. Apparently, it didn't matter that he'd never flown planes before or that the one flight I remember us all taking, to Florida, my dad was more interested in watching *Six Days, Seven Nights* than in the view outside or the hum of the engine. A few dozen hours up in a Cessna, and *voilà*—pilot. Soon after, we moved into a house with four bedrooms and a backyard with two oak trees that are the perfect distance apart for holding up the hammock we're going to get in the spring.

Mom and Dad's voices from the kitchen faded into the background as I went to work on the DS. I was getting near the end of Pokéman Diamond and Pearl, the best Pokéman game yet. If I played until bedtime, I could probably win. But after only a few minutes, I noticed my mind wandering. I had what felt like an itch inside my forehead that I couldn't scratch. I kept thinking about how maybe the rough days Dad mentioned from time to time weren't actually all that rough—not when you compared them to what Ted Wolff's dad must be dealing with. Ted's dad is a marine in Afghanistan. *His boots are on the ground*, Ted likes to remind me and everyone. This is his dad's third tour of duty, and Ted hasn't seen him in eleven months. I'll admit it: Sometimes I'm jealous. Every day, Ted wonders if he and his mom will receive tragic news. They still live on the base, surrounded by people who worry about them. When people pray for our troops, it's Ted's dad, not mine, they're praying for.

Mornings on the school bus, Ted tells me about his nightmares, grisly scenes straight out of a first-person shooter. Sometimes I think he makes them up to shock me, but other times I'm not so sure. His schoolwork is suffering. That's the word his teachers use and therefore he uses—"suffering"—as if Ted's notebooks and quizzes are connected to tubes and life-support systems. And he's gotten into trouble at recess for fighting—suspended twice this year. What would I get suspended for? What would I be acting out against? My dad brings home Chick-fil-A on Mondays, when Mom has ice-skating. Weekends, he makes Western omelets. He coaches my basketball team.

My dad's boots? They're on the front hall mat beside the purple lunch cooler that he brags about finding on mega-sale at Costco. On field trip days, he lets me borrow the cooler. It really does keep the hot stuff hot and the cold stuff cold.

Okay, I decide. Maybe killing a dog could be tragic. I like dogs. In two years, when I'm fifteen and my sister isn't a baby anymore, we're going to *get* a dog. And if that dog were ever to escape and run into a car's path . . . yeah. That would be a rough day for me, and for the driver, too, unless he was totally heartless. A dead dog in Afghanistan is just as dead as a dead dog in New Jersey. That's something else I've been thinking about—how it isn't the dog's fault that its owner is a terrorist. I mean, that doesn't make the *dog* a terrorist. It just makes it an unlucky dog—for having a terrorist for an owner, and for stepping in the path of a Hellfire missile.

I had those deep thoughts while playing the DS, and I'm still having them now as my dad loses his cities one by one. He's wincing, his face too serious for Atari, and I consider letting him win. But I'm already too far ahead for that. And from the look of things, he won't be completing this level, anyway. It's just as well. He wouldn't want me throwing the game. He's more interested in playing fairly and trying hard than in winning or losing. It's the coach in him. The coach that doesn't win many games.

"I'm in big trouble, boy," my dad says. "These lines are coming at me too fast!"

I almost correct him—they're *missiles*, not lines—but don't, because he's right. They don't look anything like missiles. The fact is, no one should be stuck playing an Atari 2600. But Dad was saying before Christmas how he wasn't allowed to play video games as a kid, and so Mom won him a console off eBay. She didn't know she should have bid on a Nintendo—that Atari was even before *his* time. Not only are the graphics amazingly bad, but the joystick only has one button. One!

But here's the thing: Missile Command is all right. It's actually creepier than anything on the Xbox or PlayStation. When you lose and the aliens have flattened all your cities, the words THE END appear on the screen in huge letters. Not *game over*, but THE END. Those words mean business. It almost feels like it could actually be the end of the world, until you remember that the game is from 1980 and that the world is still here.

My dad grunts as his remaining cities get squashed. But he's a good sport and waits around for me to clear level after level. I get into some sort of crazy zone and it's my best game ever. Dad is kicked back on the sofa, arms behind his head. He's actually smiling, as if the most amazing thing he's seen in his whole life is me, his son, calmly defending our pixelated planet.

"What's it like," I ask him the next afternoon on our way to the game, "flying the planes and dropping bombs and stuff?" I've never thought to ask before. Does a dentist's son ask his dad what it's like to drill a tooth? But yesterday in homeroom Ted Wolff was telling other kids that my dad wasn't a real pilot, and I told Ted he was crazy, because what else do you call someone who flies planes and bombs people? And as I said it, it occurred to me that, whoa—he bombs people.

"Ain't a pilot if he can't get blown apart," Ted said.

"That only makes him smart," I said, emphasizing that last word and immediately regretting it. I didn't mean to imply that his old man was dumb for having his boots on the ground, but that's how it sounded. If I were anybody else, Ted would've murdered me on the spot. Instead, he only got a hurt look and told me to screw off, which I immediately did. We were best friends back when our families both lived on the base. It isn't a very large base, and few kids at school come from military families and know what it's like having to prove yourself to a whole new set of kids every time your family is transferred. So it's good to stick together, look out for one another in case there's any trouble.

Mom says that Ted *is* trouble—and I guess she's right if trouble is Italian for really, really good at basketball. Thankfully, we aren't playing the Jaguars today. We're up against the Tigers. We're the Pumas. There are eight teams in the league, and six of them are cats.

Dad drives slowly through the school parking lot, as if he didn't hear my question. I don't even know why I felt compelled to ask it, except that Ted's accusation is still sitting in my stomach like bad tacos. I think I know why he said it, too: Yesterday, six marines died when their helicopter crashed in the Helmand province. That's where his father is. He wasn't hurt, but still—the man is creeping through hostile territory seven thousand miles away. I can't imagine my own father being there in the thick of combat. Where would he keep his fountain pens? But even if I could imagine my dad in Afghanistan, I know I wouldn't want him there, not if the other choice is staying here, staying safe.

My dad stops the car for some kid who's dribbling his basketball and not looking where he's going. Then he starts driving again. "Jeremy, I don't. . ." He shakes his head and starts again. "Ninety-nine percent of what I do is nothing." He goes on to say that he and his copilot watch the monitors as the remotely piloted aircraft makes passes over the enemy. "We observe," he says. "We take photographs and report what we see. To tell you the truth, it's pretty boring most of the time. We almost never engage the enemy."

"Yeah, but when you do. What's that like?"

"What's it like?" Anger has crept into his voice. "What do you *think* it's like?" This is what happens when our translator has to take Avery to Kindermusik.

Dad pulls the car into the nearest parking space. It's the same school I go to Monday through Friday but less dreary without the teachers. All around us, excited kids are rushing ahead of their parents toward the gym. Half these kids will lose today. I don't think my father meant for me to answer his question, but I really want to know and don't see myself bringing up the subject again anytime soon. "I don't know what it's like," I tell him. "That's why I'm asking."

We're in the parking space, but the engine is still idling. "I have a duty," he says, looking ahead at the windshield even though the only thing to see is the tinted windshield of the SUV facing us. He voice sounds different—deeper than normal, flatter, almost as if he's directing his words to someone other than me. "I execute the duty."

He shuts off the engine and yanks up the parking brake.

The middle-school gym has two basketball courts, which means four teams play simultaneously. With all the kids yelling and the coaches yelling and the parents yelling, it's complete mayhem, and above all that yelling is the sound of sneakers squeaking on the polished wooden floor. And four simultaneous games means a lot of refs blowing whistles, especially when the refs are high-school JV and varsity players who love reminding us how much they know about the rules.

Our games aren't long—six-minute quarters. Halfway into the second quarter we're down by ten and pretty confident it's only going to get worse. I'm sitting on the bench, already thinking about our game next week against the 0-7 Bobcats, when I see Ted standing by the water fountain wearing jeans and a hoodie, even though his team is playing right now on the other court. I nod in his direction and he catches my eye and nods back, takes one hand out of the hoodie, and motions for me to go over there.

I can't. I'm on the bench during a game. This should be obvious, so I shrug at him and stay where I am. But at halftime he's still there and motions me over again, so I tell my dad that I need to talk to Ted a second.

"The game's still on," my dad says. "We can't all be—"

"I know, but it's really important." And maybe because Ted is trouble but I'm not, my dad says okay but make it quick. Everyone else mills around the bench, drinking paper cups of Gatorade.

The water fountain where Ted is standing hasn't

worked in years. One hand is stuffed deep into his pocket, and the fingers of his other hand are flicking the side of the metal fountain.

"You guys are getting killed," he says.

"Very perceptive," I say. "How come you aren't playing?"

"My mom won't let me," he says.

"Why not?"

"Punishment. I'm failing everything."

"But she let you come and watch?"

"She made me tell Mr. Meltzer in person." He shrugs. "Kind of embarrassing, but I guess it's fair. Anyway, I want to ask you a question."

"Okay."

"Do you think you can help me pass my classes?"

"You mean cheat?"

He laughs out loud. "No, you idiot—I mean, will you tutor me?"

"Oh." I'm not the best student, but I'm not even close to the worst. I feel a flash of pride that he's chosen me—even if his mom made him—especially after what I said yesterday. "What subject?"

"Read my lips: *I'm failing everything*. Take your pick." He leans against the water fountain and crosses one sneakered foot casually in front of the other.

Ted is more than half a year older than I am. He's a head taller, has the beginnings of a moustache, and has already had girlfriends and dumped them. I get the sense that he doesn't mind being here, causing others to look at him in his street clothes and wonder.

"We can start with history. That's my best subject." Ever since I was a kid, I seemed to know more about Ronald Reagan and Mikhail Gorbachev than I ever knew about Elmo and Thomas the Train.

"History." He turns the word around in his mouth as if it's a food he's never tasted before. "Yeah, okay."

Over by the bench, my team huddles with my dad, who is tapping his clipboard and revealing the secret to our amazing second-half turnaround.

"Listen," I say to Ted. "I'm sorry about yesterday. I know it must suck having your dad away for so long."

He shakes his head. "Forget it—my dad's an asshole. Trust me, everything's a lot better when he's overseas."

"For real?"

"Of course."

His confession makes me uncomfortable—it's too candid, too honest—and the only thing I can think to do is reveal something in return. "Well, my dad practically cried at dinner last night over bombing a dog."

Ted squints a little. "He did?"

"I mean, there were no actual tears, but—"

"No, I mean the dog. He said he did that?"

"Yeah, but it was an accident."

"I'm talking about his words—he said he killed a dog?"

"Um, that's what I just said."

Ted shakes his head. "Oh, man, that's no good."

"What do you mean?"

He waits a second, then leans in and lowers his voice. "That's *code*, man. Your dad killed a kid." He sucks in his breath, lets it out. "When they kill a kid, they call it a dog."

"Screw off," I tell him.

"I'm sorry, Jeremy, but they do."

"You don't know what the hell you're talking about."

"It's common knowledge on the base."

The base. It's true, you hear things on the base—in the commissary, the laundromat, the exchange—that you don't hear anywhere else. "Why would they call it that?"

The look he gives me makes me feel like he's twice my age. "Think about it, man. You blow the arms and legs off a kid, you'd better start thinking of it as a dog in a hurry."

My dad, in his ironed khakis and button-down white shirt, is still on his haunches, motivating the team. In a couple of minutes the refs will blow their whistles and the second half will start. My dad will call out which five of us will take the floor, not that it matters. He'll give us all equal time. He catches my gaze and flashes a smile so quick and knowing, it seems to say, *Take your time with Ted. He's in trouble and needs your help.* But when I turn back to Ted to say forget it, find another damn tutor, he's already on his way out of the gym.

My vision gets swimmy. My skin feels like it isn't my skin. Two years ago, when we were living on the base, I caught my mother smoking a cigarette behind the apartment, and it was as if my universe had twisted inside-out. All I was ever told about smoking—at school, at home—was that it killed you, and here she was killing herself. She swore she wasn't a smoker, that it was only occasional, a rare lapse, swore it up and down, but the secret she'd been keeping from me (for years? my whole life?) felt heavy as a meteor and all I could think was, *You aren't you. You're somebody else.* It took me months to get past it, or maybe I still haven't gotten past it.

But this. Does my father really kill children? Is that his job? Was it even an accident? What if it had been me living in Afghanistan? Would he have bombed me? Would he have done it sadly? Gladly? Would he have lied about it afterward, said I was a dog? I have no idea who my father is and no idea what to do: leave the building and go after Ted? Go someplace else? Go where? I'm trying to figure out what the hell I should be doing right now with these useless hands and this skin that isn't mine when I hear a harsh whistle—not a ref's whistle but the piercing, three-fingered hoot of all coaches. "Jeremy!" my father shouts. "Shake a leg, will you?"

So I shake a leg and let myself be coached into a season-high eight points. Despite the other team's insurmountable lead, I play so hard on both ends of the floor that when the game ends and I throw up in the bathroom, it's possible that it was from giving it my all.

I say as little as possible on the drive home and endure a supper of my mother asking for a play-by-play of the game and my dad asking what it was that Ted wanted, then the two of them being so proud of me for agreeing to become Ted's tutor. When I'm finally excused, I go upstairs and cry in my bedroom, a kid into his pillow. I stay there, pretending to rest, pretending to read, then really reading, then playing the DS. Eventually my father comes by my room, as I know he will, and asks how my thumbs are feeling.

I tell him not tonight. I tell him I'm tired.

"You played well today," he says.

"Thanks," I say. "Dad?"

He's standing in the doorway looking tired, as if he was out there on the court earlier.

"What kind of dog was it?" I ask.

He takes a moment, as if figuring out what I'm referring to. "Is this a for-real question?"

"Yeah," I say.

He looks at me some more. "It was mid-sized, Jeremy. Brown. Short-haired." It's darker in the hall than in my bedroom, and I can't tell if his eyes are focused on me or above my head, looking at something that isn't there. "Probably some kind of hound, if I had to guess," he says, and I can't help picturing a boy about my size. "Big ears," he says, and that boy's ears are poking out from his head, same as mine do, a boy with a new haircut. He takes a breath. "Well, good-night, son."

Maybe I say good-night; maybe I don't. He walks away, down the hall toward his bedroom, leaving me to picture the animal he described in so much detail that it brings me no comfort, no assurance.

You're so full of crap, I say under my breath—to my father, to Ted—way too softly for anyone to hear. But what if they aren't? It would mean that my mother isn't the only translator in the family, that my father takes what he sees on his monitor and turns it into something that he can live with, if not understand. It isn't fair play. It makes all play unfair.

When he shuts the door I pick up the DS and kill time until everyone else goes to sleep. It takes a while. The moment the crack under my parents' door goes dark, Avery starts crying in the nursery, and so my mother gets up and heads off to feed and hold her until she burps.

Then she comes into my room. "Are you still awake?" I had the covers pulled up over my head so she wouldn't see the light coming from the game. "How'd you know?"

"All the clicking."

It occurs to me that I need to start sleeping with my bedroom door shut. "I just want to win the game. I'm really close." The truth is, I finished it this morning before soccer. I'm just breezing through the early levels again to pass the time.

"You can win tomorrow," she says.

"Can I ask you something?"

"You just did." An automatic response—we do that all the time. But then my mattress shifts as she sits on the edge of my bed, and I ask her if Dad likes being a pilot.

"The truth? We don't talk about it much." She's practically whispering. Even I can tell the difference between not wanting to wake anybody and not wanting anyone to hear.

"I thought you guys tell each other everything."

"Yeah, well. Communicating is what a historian does," she says. "Your father flies planes now."

When she first came into the room, I considered asking her about the dog—what it means or might mean. I wanted answers. I wanted company. I wanted my mother to tell me that there's nothing to panic about. But the way she's talking—it isn't like her. Nothing's like anybody. So I ask if I can keep playing the DS a while longer, so that she'll be able to keep telling herself that my greatest concern is Pokéman.

"Five more minutes." Then she says *buona notte* and kisses the top of my head, which makes me feel like I'm half my age, but then again that's what I was going for, and I retract, turtle-like, back under the covers.

After my mother goes back to bed, I wait until the house has been quiet for some time, and then I sneak downstairs, where I stare at the TV screen and, with the lights off and the volume low, begin to defend my cities. I want to feel whatever it is my father feels, and I imagine that the missiles raining down on me are real ICBMs and MIRVs. The cities I'm defending are real, too: New York, Philadelphia, Chicago. Then I take it further, imagining that each city is actually an entire country: Australia, England, America, etc. Every human soul, and I'm responsible for them all.

Yet the more real I try to make it, the worse my score. So the next game, I remind myself that I'm shooting at slanty lines. That I'm defending blobs of pixels. I'm playing a simple game, a game for kids, nothing more, created long before an on-screen explosion meant anything more than it was your buddy's turn. And almost at once, my breathing eases, my thumbs and wrists relax. I'm seriously locked in—with the game, with my father—and I stay on the loveseat, postponing THE END late into the night, through another level, and another level, and another.

Star to the East

Maya's husband, Steve, was a YouTube prankster for a living. It wasn't something he'd planned—no one planned such a career then—but rather the result of one video going viral accidentally, then another deliberately. Before long he had mastered what he called the "secret sauce." He and Maya were both a couple of years out of the Midwestern state university where they had been honors students on scholarship. After graduation, the Coffee Countdown agreed to increase Maya's hours to full time, and she started volunteering at the local animal shelter. Steve proposed. And soon they were a newly married couple and the adoptive parents of a kindhearted, droopy-jowled rescue hound they named Woof Blitzer. They didn't have much money, Maya and Steve, but they didn't need it, and they were keenly aware of how rare and fortunate this was, to be carefree and in no one's debt.

They didn't want children. More precisely, Steve was infertile—the result of the radiation used to obliterate a frightening childhood tumor—and neither he nor Maya wanted children enough to see his infertility as something other than a sign of what was meant to be. So their needs were few, and Maya's café gig plus the ad revenue from Steve's videos brought in enough money to justify putting off, for a while, more serious plans, such as Maya's matriculation into graduate school for social work, or Steve's entry into the industry for which he had trained, which was healthcare administration.

They lived together in a modest, three-bedroom rental house in a subdivision of modest ranch houses. The smallest bedroom was full of Steve's gear: computers and sound mixers and boom stands and lighting. Another bedroom belonged to their niece, Edie, with her drawings on the walls, her princess castle in the corner, her CD player for her music. Maya and Steve wouldn't themselves be parents but had made a point, ever since the girl's birth, to throw themselves into their roles as Aunt Maya and Uncle Steve to this blonde-haired, blue-eyed force of nature with the impressive *port de bras* and an even better stink-eye. When Edie's parents were unable to take her to dance class or to chaperone a school trip, Maya or Steve would do it. They were the go-to babysitters—they insisted on it—and often it was just easier and more fun for Edie to spend the night.

On Tuesdays, Maya didn't go in to the café until 11 a.m., and June, her sister, would drop by Maya's house for breakfast on her way to the bank where she worked as a home mortgage specialist. Steve, never an early riser, would be catching up on a little sleep and giving the two sisters some time to themselves.

"Edie was right," June said this morning, while Maya poured their coffee. "That woman is the worst."

Lately, the topic of conversation was often Edie's first grade teacher. From the way June talked, Miss

Clarkson was a real pill. Edie had been complaining each morning before school that her stomach hurt. But all June's information had come secondhand. Last night had been parent-teacher conferences, and June finally had gotten a chance to speak directly with the teacher.

"Did you bring up the ducks?" Maya asked.

Last week the kids had drawn pictures of ducks. But some of the kids forgot to write their names on their duck pictures before handing them in. Miss Clarkson, if Edie was to be believed, had held up each picture without a name (Edie's was one), torn it in half, and dropped it into the trashcan.

"Edie was telling the truth," June said. "When I asked about it, Miss Clarkson said, 'It's very important they learn to follow directions.'"

"Wow."

"Yeah, wow. I'm telling you, the woman's a nut. She told us Edie's been *defiant* in class."

"Bullshit," Maya said. Edie was a good kid, and polite.

"When I asked for specifics, she told me about a time when a kid in Edie's reading group got in trouble and Edie took the kid's side."

"Wait a minute." Maya set her cup down. "So her example of Edie being defiant was her showing empathy toward another student?"

"Yup."

"Good lord."

"See what we're dealing with? I swear, something is *wrong* with that woman."

That was possible. Or maybe the teacher was inexperienced and intimidated or going through a divorce or someone she loved was horribly ill. Maya wanted to say, *Don't you remember what we were like when Mom was dying?* June had been pregnant at the time. It had been Maya's senior year in college. She'd gone from As to Cs. She'd drunk too much. Temporarily broken up with Steve. The best of us, Maya believed, hid our suffering poorly. Though it was also possible that Miss Clarkson wasn't suffering, that she simply had chosen a career that didn't suit her.

"Can't you do anything about it?" Maya asked.

"Do what? They don't let you change classes. If it gets bad enough, I guess we'll go to the principal, who will do nothing." She looked out the window. All the leaves were super-saturated in reds and yellows, still hanging on. Autumn was one windy storm away from its back stretch. "Maybe. I don't know. I feel like there's something we should be doing. . ." She sighed. "Maya, I swear, parenting is just one failure after another."

And there was the great divide, made plain by June's declaration as to what parenting fundamentally *was*—and all Maya could do was smile as if she, too, knew. But of course she didn't know what parenting was or if she would agree with her sister about failure's prime position in its hierarchy. Maya had learned these past six years that when June became philosophical about parenting, it was better not to weigh in. Even for Maya to voice her own ignorance was to commit a tactical error, leading to June's sermonizing about how much easier and pressure-free life was when you weren't a parent and time was your own and you were responsible only for yourself. Maya and June had always been close, but sometimes being close meant knowing when to avoid taking the bait. She patted her sister's hand and got up to refresh their mugs.

"You know what she said at the end of our conference?" June said moments later, her hands warming on the refilled mug.

"What's that?" Maya asked.

"If we ever needed a babysitter, we should keep her in mind."

Maya laughed.

"Here." June removed a rectangle of paper from her purse and handed it to Maya. "She asked if I'd mind hanging this up at the bank."

Maya unfolded the paper.

> *Licensed teacher available for babysitting. Experienced teacher with CPR certification. Pet sitting too!*

The flier had those little tear-off tabs at the bottom with "Brooke" and a phone number in tiny print.

"Keep it," June said when Maya went to hand the flier back. "I don't need it."

The two sisters walked to the door. They hugged and June left, and no sooner had Maya returned to the kitchen than Steve emerged from the bedroom. He had on blue jeans and no shirt, and was toweling off his mop of shaggy hair. "That teacher sounds like a disaster."

"You caught some of that?" Maya asked. "I thought you were sleeping."

"I was," he said, "then I wasn't."

"It would've been fine if you came out."

"I didn't want to interrupt." He laid the towel over the back of a kitchen chair and kissed Maya. "Sounds like a lousy situation."

Maya agreed.

"But. . ." He looked at the flier on the kitchen table.

"But what?"

"Nothing. It's just that we have someone in the family who maybe can help."

At first, Maya was unsure what he meant. The nature of his grin made her surer. "No," she said.

His grin was devious but lovely. "He happens to be an expert on getting even."

"Forget it."

"I think you know him, too. Boyish charm, handsome penis. . ."

She was shaking her head. "Absolutely not."

"I'm thinking a simple prank is just the thing." Then in his talking-to-the-dog voice he said, "*Come here, little Woofy! You come here right now, little man. . .*"

The dog trotted over, tail flipping back and forth. He rolled over, and Steve knelt down and scratched the dog's belly. Then he stood up and looked at the flier again. "Maybe it should involve the dog. He's kind of a freeloader, when you think about it. *Aren't you, Woofy? Yes, you are, my little freeloader!* Actually, I'm having this eureka moment."

"Steve, what you're having is called a terrible idea."

"No, wait a second—okay, I've got it." He clapped his hands together, and the dog startled and sat up straight.

"Just like that?" Maya asked.

"It's what I do, my love."

Steve's first viral video wasn't a prank but rather an accident caught on tape. He and Maya had traveled east to New Jersey for Thanksgiving and were staying with one of Steve's cousins who lived in a condo by a lake. There was a backyard, between the condo and the lake, where Steve and the kids were playing Wiffle ball. A long hit sent Steve running backwards until he found himself disappearing, limbs thrashing, off a low retaining wall and into the water.

That by itself had been humorous (though only afterward, when it was clear he hadn't been hurt). But what happened next accounted for the million views. Steve's cousin, who happened to have recorded the fall on her phone, kept recording as she ran toward the water. Steve sprang up, soaked, embarrassed, saying, "I'm okay!" just as a huge gray goose appeared from a patch of nearby cattails. The goose was pissed. It ran, wings spread, head down and honking, straight for Steve, who barely had time to turn around before the belt buckle of his pants was suddenly in the animal's beak. Then came fifteen seconds of Steve flailing, panicked, scrambling up the retaining wall with a determined goose attached to his clothes, and his cousin, off-camera, shouting panicked, wildly colorful obscenities at the goose.

It was the goose, Steve would come to say, that laid

the golden egg. In the two years after, he created more than thirty videos of men and women finding themselves "goosed." His pranks were sometimes as simple as a nurse's encounter with a nest of fake rats under a patient's bedsheets, but they were often impressive, uncomfortable orchestrations involving the help of a victim's boss or spouse or friends, or a cop with a sense of humor.

Once he had a track record, recruiting confederates became easier. And Steve proved himself to be a talented prankster but an equally talented videographer, editor, and social media optimizer. The finished videos were usually very funny and sometimes shocking, though never too shocking. He knew where to draw the line. And this, too, was a talent, though whenever he got interviewed for someone's blog or pop culture website, he was dependably self-deprecating. *I have no more abilities than that shrieking goose*, he was fond of saying.

But the truth was, it was never about the goose. The appeal of that first video, what made it necessary to stop whatever you were doing and watch, was Steve's reaction to the goose emerging, irate, from the cattails and hooking itself to his clothing. Steve's brief terror caught on video was a thing of absolute honesty. It was real, and strangely intimate, a sort of pornography that people could watch in public and feel good about sharing with friends and coworkers. And Steve had put this insight to work with his YouTube channel, Hanky Pranky, which quickly bloomed like a flower.

Whatever embarrassment Maya initially felt about her husband's upstart business had long since faded. So what if his training was in business administration and accounting with a focus on the healthcare industry? The healthcare industry wasn't going anywhere. And in the meantime, who loved his job? Who gave millions around the world a moment of pleasure, a brief break in a long day? Who had created something out of nothing? Without ever meaning to, Steve had taught

Maya that when something amazing falls into your lap, you don't ask questions. You go with it.

Their niece's teacher, though. No, that wouldn't be a good idea. This teacher didn't sound as if she had a sense of humor. What if she took it badly? Worse, what if it came out somehow that Edie was the prankster's niece? June would never forgive them, because Edie could be the one to pay the price. The way June talked, this teacher could be exactly the sort of person to make a kid suffer for a crime she had nothing to do with. And it was only October. There were a lot of school days left.

So she told Steve no. She told him that morning, and again that night when she came home from the café. Pranking their niece's teacher might be fun to think about, but he shouldn't seriously consider doing it. She explained why. He listened to her. Then he said, "I don't tell you how to make a latte"—which was very snarky and not a nice way to behave when you're naked, which they were. They were naked kind of a lot, one of the perks of childlessness and Steve's flexible schedule.

"Say you're sorry," she said. He knew that Maya was sensitive about her barista gig—the "for now" job that had gone on too long.

He kissed her and apologized.

Though to be fair, Maya thought, he happened to be right. Pranking—whom to choose, what to do—was his area of expertise. Maybe it wasn't Maya's place to defend this teacher, regardless of what motivated her behavior: nastiness or pain, personality or situation.

Ultimately, once they were dressed again and had left the bedroom and were bumming around on their computers, they compromised. Steve would prank this teacher, Miss Clarkson, but it would go unrecorded. Forget viral videos. Forget sharing with the world. The woman herself would never even know she'd been pranked. This would be, as Steve explained it, "solely for the love of the art form."

"And you can't ever tell June," she said.

"Do you think I'm crazy?"

Maya smiled. "I absolutely think you're crazy," she said, and then she opened up the calendar program on her computer and the two of them decided which night they would choose for their date.

She had to admit it was a clever prank, though crueler than anything she would have imagined herself agreeing to taking part in. Maybe that was why they fit so well together, she and Steve. He was the id, she the superego. Or something like that.

The evening when Ms. Clarkson was slated to dogsit wasn't for another two weeks. And in that time, Edie's teacher remained, in the eyes of her mother, public enemy number one. (Though that was to be expected: once a person got on June's bad side, they tended to stay there.)

Knowing Maya's ambivalence, Steve took care of all the logistics—the crate that Woof Blitzer hadn't spent time in since they'd first taken him home from the shelter, the fake dog medicine (water with food coloring), the typed-out instructions. That night, the dog made himself at home on the bed while Maya selected a necklace to go with her black dress. She brushed her hair and put on lipstick. Steve looked great in his rarely worn gray blazer, linen pants, and black wingtips.

The doorbell rang precisely at 8:30. Woof Blitzer barked twice, jumped off the bed, and trotted down the hallway. By the time Maya got to the foyer, Steve had already opened the front door, and their niece's teacher was stepping into the house. Maya wasn't sure what she'd been imagining (black teeth? hairy nose-wart?), but this petite young woman standing in the foyer, rubbing the cold off her hands, wasn't it.

"It feels like winter already!" the teacher said to them, smiling. Her teeth were perfect. Nose: unblemished. Eyes wide and alert. "I'm so glad to meet you both." She introduced herself—"I'm Brooke. Your house is lovely"—and shook their hands. She knelt down to the dog. "And you must be the patient." Woof Blitzer, typically slow to warm to strangers, flopped down at her feet to be petted.

This was all wrong, Maya thought as Steve took the teacher's coat and hung it in the closet. He led them into the kitchen, and Woof Blitzer followed, tail wagging. Steve gave the teacher instructions about when to let the dog outside into the fenced-in backyard, when and how to administer the medicine. Ms. Clarkson—Brooke—nodded, making sure she knew just what do to.

"Don't worry," she said. "Your pup and I are going to have a good time."

Wrong. All wrong. The plan was to let the dog into the backyard alone before they left, and then Steve would sneak around the side, quietly open the gate, and get the dog. They would put him into their car and drive away. At some point, maybe thirty minutes or an hour later, the teacher would call Maya's cell with the mortifying news that the dog was missing. A cruel prank worthy of a cruel subject—which Brooke Clarkson, it just seemed, was not.

Maya asked, "So what grade do you teach?"

"First."

"Wow—that's an important year."

"Tell me about it," she said. "The kids are such sponges at that age, and I want to do a good job, you know?"

Maya shot a quick glance at Steve, who said he was going to let the dog out into the backyard. He clapped his hands twice, said "C'mere, boy," and the dog followed him out of the room.

"I'll bet the kids can be a handful," Maya said. She felt a little desperate to start disliking this apparently normal person who was, quite possibly, the victim of her sister's unfair wrath.

"I've learned you have to run a tight ship." Maya was wondering if there was any possible way to get her talking about ducks and anonymous drawings when

Brooke lowered her voice. "Really, I think what makes it hard is they're so stupid."

Maya's eyes widened. "Sorry?"

"Okay"—she flashed that beautiful smile—"not stupid maybe. That sounds cruel. Let's just say ignorant. And sort of hopeless. You can tell even at that age who's going to amount to anything."

Thank you for this gift, Maya thought as her guilt began sliding off her like a constricting layer of skin. "Is that so?"

"Oh, absolutely."

"How can you tell?"

"You just can. You can tell by looking at them, and I'm not being racist at all."

Okay, Brooke, that's enough now.

"For real," Brooke went on. "One of my blonde girls, she looks like a princess but, goodness, is she a brat and dumb as a stump. No light in her eyes at all. The girl can't even remember to put her name on her drawings."

"Is that so?"

"Of course her mother thinks she walks on water. Hey, can I be honest?" Maya wasn't sure she wanted any more honesty from Brooke. A surplus of honesty wasn't necessary. But before she could reply, Brooke said, "Everyone talks about the education crisis? But really it's a parenting crisis. You're Christian, aren't you?"

Maya nodded, pretty sure she knew where this was going.

"Well, I'm teaching these children to be good Christians and future leaders, and meanwhile parents are teaching them to hate the police and love the terrorists. It's all backwards." She shrugged. "But this is what happens when you take Jesus out of the classroom." Brooke's face was sunshine and rainbows and sweet tea.

"Excuse me a moment," Maya said. She went to the kitchen, got herself a glass of water, and drank it.

"You about ready?" Steve asked, entering the kitchen.

Maya put the class into the sink. "Go get the dog."

"What do you mean?" He widened his eyes, silently reminding Maya that Brooke was only in the next room and could probably hear every word. "Woofy loves being outside—"

"Trust me," Maya said. "You need to get him back inside. Now. And I need another minute to finish getting ready." She went down the hallway and into Edie's bedroom, where she turned on the nightlight and the white-noise machine. She unmade the bed, and on her way out she silently shut the door behind her.

Steve had let Woof Blitzer back into the house, and the dog lay sprawled on the living room sofa. Brooke was petting him, and Steve stood beside them, not too visibly sulking from having his prank derailed.

"So Brooke," Maya said, "it's very unlikely that Audrey will wake up, because she gets her best sleep early in the night. But if she does—"

Brooke was watching curiously. So was Steve. "I'm sorry. Who?" Brooke asked.

"Well, our *daughter*, of course." She put a hand on Steve's arm. "Tell me you only mentioned the dog." He stood, frozen. Maya rolled her eyes and laughed. "Typical. God, Steve, do you mean you didn't mention the *human* when you—?" She shook her head. "Well, to be fair, the dog *is* more trouble." More head-shaking. "Second door on the left—but you shouldn't have to do anything. If she wakes up, just pat her on the back. She still wears diapers at night, so you can change her if she's wet, but honestly that's probably more trouble than it's worth because usually in the first part of the night she sleeps great. But do me a favor?"

"Um, sure," Brooke said, glancing at Steve and then back at Maya. "Okay."

"I always tuck the blanket under the mattress so she can't pull it up over her head, but it still makes me nervous. SIDS and all that. Would you mind just checking on her in about an hour? I know that makes me sound a little paranoid."

"No—of course. It's no problem."

"Can you think of anything else, Steve?" Maya asked.

He was gazing at her in awe or maybe horror or deep admiration. "No, I think that pretty much covers it."

They went to the coat closet, which Maya opened only partway because the door squeaked a little. She got her coat and handed Steve his, smiled at the sitter, and then she said goodbye to the dog. She and Steve left the house, Maya closing the door gently behind them. By the time they were in the car, she was shaking badly. "I think I'm going to throw up," she said.

Steve started the engine and they sat facing forward with the car idling. "This isn't a minor prank, sweetie."

"No."

"What if she calls 9-1-1 before calling us?"

"I need a drink badly. Will you take me somewhere to get a drink?"

He looked at her. "We could go back inside. We'll send her home. She'll never know."

"Just drive."

"It's just that . . . a child. Missing."

Maya could practically hear the air crackling around her. It was terrifying, what they were doing, but she felt giddy at the prospect of going all the way—over a retaining wall, a cliff, anywhere.

"I'm begging you to drive, Steve. Please let's just fucking go."

He left his hands on the wheel another moment before shifting into reverse, backing out of the driveway, and starting down their quiet street. He turned onto the main road. As he drove, Maya watched out the window. It was a clear night. The western sky behind them was still twilight but the eastern sky ahead was dark, and there were stars that formed constellations that Maya maybe knew in her childhood but had long since forgotten. A bright star was directly ahead and seemed almost to beckon them, though maybe it was only a planet.

Soon she and Steve were seated on adjacent barstools at the Beetle Bar, a quiet, dark place with overpriced drinks to keep the college kids away. They barely spoke as the minutes ticked past. Maya's phone lay on the bar between them. As the hour drew to a close, her heart thudded. The two gin and tonics had maybe helped a little, but not enough. Steve told her he always felt this way when the prank was on, but his voice gave him away. He wasn't enjoying it either. He was scared. After another ten minutes, Maya began to wonder if maybe the sitter had forgotten to check the bedroom. Or maybe she'd decided it was better to leave a sleeping child alone than risk waking her. If that were the case, then she and Steve could race home, pay the sitter, and wash their hands of this. Which was what they should do. This dread was not worth anything. Nor was the cruelty. So what if Brooke Clarkson was a lousy teacher? What did it matter, really, in the life of their happy, well-adjusted niece? Maya waited another few seconds, waiting for the call, dreading the call, before realizing that she could end it now. She could simply phone the sitter and say, On second thought, don't check on the child.

As she picked up the phone, it buzzed and a text appeared.

Sender: Brooke Clarkson.

> *Just wanted to let you know that Audrey is sleeping great. Dog is fine too. Take ur time and have fun.*

Maya stared at her phone.

"What?" Steve asked. She handed him the phone and then he stared at it awhile. He handed it back. "She's playing us."

"Yeah."

"I wonder how she—" He shook his head. "Huh."

"I almost respect how much I hate her," Maya said, and then she looked at her phone again, though the screen had gone black. It was an ideal night at the Beetle Bar, populated but not crowded, a good soul mix coming through the speakers. She took a drink, put her glass down again. "She *is* pranking us, though, right?"

"Well—yeah."

"Because otherwise. . ." But Maya couldn't figure out an *otherwise*.

"Otherwise, she's insane," Steve said.

The bartender came over and asked if he'd like another.

"No, we need to settle up," Maya said. "We're in a hurry."

At home, Woof Blitzer greeted them unenthusiastically at the door before returning to the green sofa where he usually lounged at night. Brooke stretched and said, "You guys could have stayed out longer," and Maya waited for her to wink, or blink, or curse them out, or laugh. She waited for the teacher to fess up or explain, but then Steve was taking out his wallet and offering some bills and getting Brooke's coat from the coat closet, and then she left the house with a wave and an "Anytime you need someone, just holler."

Edie's bedroom door was closed. Maya and Steve stood silently outside it in the hallway. There was no reason to open the door quietly. No reason to hesitate. Yet Maya did. The room was just as it was before they had left the house. Maya had set the noise machine to "rain," the sound that Edie slept with. The nightlight emitted the dimmest glow. Maya went over to the bed. The blanket covered most of the mattress. It was pulled up to the shoulders of the little girl, about half Edie's age, who lay on her side, eyes closed and breathing deeply.

Maya reached out and grasped Steve's arm. Hoping this was all somehow part of his machinations; hoping this prank was massive and directed at her, that Brooke and Steve were in it together, doing this to Maya for reasons he would only now reveal. Hoping he was proving himself to be brilliant and sadistic, but knowing he was only a good man with a few tricks up his sleeve.

"Maya?" he whispered, perhaps hoping the same about her.

They stared at the child, who slept on.

At halftime, the music of trumpets and trombones shimmered in the sharp fall afternoon air. The marching band's polyester uniforms matched the deep blue of the cloudless sky. The thump-thump of the three bass drums and crack of the five snare drums playing in unison echoed off the brick high school in the distance and probably could be heard for a mile or more. In the bleachers, parents and siblings stretched their legs, drank hot cocoa from paper cups, reached into slender bags of popcorn.

The marching band had learned a new routine this week and already moved with practiced precision and confidence, snapping around corners, everyone in lock-step. Their prior show had been tailored for a marching band competition, and Audrey felt (and Maya agreed) that it had been too dreary for football. But today's performance was livelier. The song they were playing was a Sousa march—not "Stars and Stripes Forever," but something equally timeless and familiar. The parents who weren't chasing small children around (God, how exhausting that had been, Maya remembered) were watching the halftime show and clapping hands, tapping feet. The playing wasn't flawless but you wouldn't know it from its rousing effect, though of course much of the crowd consisted of the parents of the teenagers carrying all those horns and tubas and clarinets. And flutes. Eight flutists were out there playing their sweet hearts out, not that anyone could hear them. (Maya recalled Audrey mentioning something about the band director begging more of the girls to *just try* the piccolo.)

The band stopped moving and marched in place.

Then the musicians planted both feet on the ground so that they all faced the home bleachers, while the music came to a stirring crescendo.

Audrey stood third flutist from the left. Her light brown hair blew lightly in the breeze beneath the blue cap with a red plume sticking up. Her delicate fingers moved quickly over the instrument, creating what from halfway up the bleachers was an inaudible contribution. But then the wind suddenly shifted and a strong gust blew across the stands carrying the unmistakable, unexpected sound of flutes. Soft, like floating leaves, the runs and trills of the flutes rose above and dipped below and danced around the chorus of instruments as the march moved into its final refrain. A chill ran down Maya's spine. She gripped Steve's hand. He wore a cap because his head, balding on top, became cold easily. She was glad he'd come. Since his promotion to director of client services, his Saturdays were often spent at the office catching up on work.

He turned toward Maya. "I think I can hear her!"

They still had no idea who the hell this girl was. This child, this terrifying miracle who had appeared in Edie's bed. And now thirteen years had come and gone, those first interminable hours and days yielding to faster weeks and months, somehow becoming years that blinked by as quickly, it seemed, as a camera's flash.

Maya held her husband's hand. Seized by panic, she watched the field: the band, the baton and rifles twirlers, the drum major at the fifty-yard line conducting with gloved hands. After all this time, the chance of Audrey being taken from them had to be less. Still, her terror never abated for long, and always it came back like a tsunami, crashing into her at unexpected moments, leaving Maya breathless and drowning.

After three or four seconds the wind shifted again. The flutes were subsumed by the other instruments, and the music of her daughter was gone.

Animals

It's nearly lunchtime and the woman on the phone is getting snippy, so I intentionally flub a word. "I know this must be fistering for you."

"I beg your pardon?" she says.

"Fistering. Fisterating?"

"Do you mean 'frustrating'?"

"Yes—I mean that. I use the wrong word sometimes," I tell her, just as I've been taught to say. My confession will cause her temper to subside.

"But your English is really quite good," she says.

"Thank you," I tell her. "You are kind."

"It's the truth, Raj. Have you ever been to America?" She calls me Raj because she believes it's my name. Because I told her it is.

"No, Josephine," I tell her. That's her name—Josephine Sanders. "Though one of my cousins attends UCLA. He likes America very much."

I know nothing about this woman other than her name, phone number, and computer model, but I sense she isn't a bad person. Certainly, her frustration is warranted. The CD-ROM drive on her new computer shouldn't already be failing.

"There's a lot to like," she says. "Not everything, but a lot. You should visit your cousin if you get the chance."

I thank her again and feel glad that we're being civil now.

"So tell me," the woman says, "where about in India are you guys located?" She's speaking to me as if to an acquaintance who might someday become her friend. It wouldn't be hard to convince myself that she's lonely.

I tell her that the HCC call center is located in a small city named Veraval, on India's western shoreline. "It's traditionally a fishing port," I explain, "but we are attempting to modernize."

I would never have known about that distant city's existence had it not been circled in red marker on the map handed to us at orientation. The map is tacked to my cubicle along with various memos and reminders, a photograph of my parents, and another photograph of Pongo, the Doberman Pinscher I grew up with in Red Bank, New Jersey, and who is now buried in my parents' backyard.

"Everyone tries to modernize," the woman says. "It doesn't always lead to happiness."

"I know you're right," I tell her, because we're supposed to agree with the customer whenever feasible. I then repeat my feelings of personal sorrow that the CD-ROM drive on her Handel computer has stopped whirring, and I offer another apology for being unable to get it whirring again despite the twenty minutes we've spent together on the telephone, not to mention the thirty or more that she spent on hold prior to our conversation.

"I know this must be very . . . *frustrating*," I say, as if forcing my tongue into a new, baffling position, "but if you would hold for a moment, I'll transfer you to a scheduling agent, who will schedule an appointment for a service technician in your area to come to your home."

"I'd appreciate that," she says. "I'm in the middle of writing my doctoral dissertation, and I desperately need a working computer at home."

"Really? What's your subject?" Without meaning to, I've veered off-script and spoken way too informally. But I couldn't help it. A Ph.D. takes years to obtain, and I'm always bowled over by people with the luck and stamina to see their plans through.

"Sociology," she says, apparently unaware of my change in syntax. "I'm studying workplace stress in Memphis—that's a city in Tennessee—and the way that people react to it differently across gender and racial lines."

"I know where is Memphis," I say, overdoing it a little now. "Elvis Presley. Graceland."

"That's right," she says.

But Elvis holds no interest for me. "How long have you been writing your dissertation?"

"Six months," she says. "But I've been collecting data for years. It's become my whole life."

"Your study is very important," I tell her.

"I used to think so," she says. "Now I just want it finished. I've become a horrible person to be around. At night I dream about data files. Or about murdering my dissertation director." She laughs, but I can tell she doesn't think anything is funny. "And yes, I'm aware of the irony. Do you know what I mean by that, Raj?"

Because I find myself wanting her to like me, I answer her question the way I imagine a bright, bilingual man named Raj from Veraval would: "Irony? I believe so. You are studying workplace stress, and your work is causing you stress." When I get it right—the answer, the accent, the syntax—I *feel* like Raj, an optimistic upstart from Veraval, a young and ambitious cog in the wheel of international commerce. I imagine him carrying a briefcase to work. I feel glad for him.

"You got that right, amigo." She sighs into the phone. "Look, you sound like a nice guy, but I really need that computer to work. It's kind of a big deal."

"I understand," I tell her, disappointed to be getting back on script. But it's just as well. Today is Catfish Wednesday, and on Catfish Wednesday you have to beat the crowd. My bank of cubicles abuts the employee cafeteria, and my stomach is growling in response to the deep fryer. "I'm glad to help. Thank you for calling Handel Computers, Josephine. I'll transfer you now to a scheduling agent."

And because her problem is not a Critical Operating System Error, I do exactly what I've been trained to do. I hang up on her.

Training was a two-week affair in January. That was ten months ago, when I was desperate for work. To summarize: I'd come South for veterinary school, flunked out but didn't tell my family or friends back North, then decided to stick around so I could reapply the following year as an in-state resident. The dean said my chances for readmission were 50/50, which were about the best odds I'd ever been given for anything.

On our first day at Arihant, we twenty new hires followed our team leader to a windowless classroom deep in the bowels of the building, where we learned about the telephone system and call-tracking software, and about the Handel Computer Corporation, the Seattle company that was outsourcing its customer service and tech support to us. The next two days, we received rudimentary training in PC support.

The following Monday morning began with a biscuit-and-gravy breakfast for the eighteen of us who'd made it successfully through the first week. A tall woman who looked a little like Christie Whitman rushed into the room, whammed the door shut behind her, and introduced herself as Margaret Lighthouse, our CEO. After presenting her brief biography—Wharton Business School, executive positions here and there—she handed out confidentiality statements for us to sign. Her eyes narrowed as she explained the severe repercussions of revealing company secrets—dismissal, criminal prosecution, the works.

Did she frighten any of us away? Not a chance. Not in this recession. We needed the work.

After collecting the forms, she smiled as if seeing us for the first time, shut off the lights, and began a Power Point presentation about the history of the American customer service industry. Projected onto the white screen were dry statistics about the loss of American jobs and the number of call centers being established overseas, where wages were low and employee motivation high.

"Riveting stuff," I whispered to the middle-aged woman beside me. She moved her chair away.

Margaret Lighthouse flipped on the lights, causing us all to blink and sit up a little straighter. "So now I have one of those company secrets to tell you about," she said, and winked.

Five minutes later, people were grinning. They tittered nervously. An elderly gentleman in a crisp suit muttered, "Holy shit," which caused more titters.

Fortified with an amazing secret, strong company coffee, and the knowledge that we were being paid for our time, we spent the next five days learning how to hide our natural dialects—Southern, East Coast, whatever—and to speak English with a proper Indian accent. Our teachers alternated between a retired TV meteorologist from Calcutta and a Mississippi-born linguist with a doctoral degree from Georgia State.

For eight hours a day, our instructors lectured us, grilled us, popped quizzes, and made us speak in front of the class. They assigned homework and expected us to do it. They taught us to drop our dipthongs and pronounce our W's like V's and our V's like B's. The three days devoted to phonology demanded tremendous concentration and practice. The final two days covered syntax and diction: applying plurals incorrectly, overusing gerund constructions and reflexive pronouns. And by the end of the week, my classmates sounded, to my ears anyway, less like residents of northern Mississippi and more like native Hindi speakers with an impressive command of the English language.

And if we could fool me, then surely we could fool some fed-up customer in the American heartland.

The con—there's no other word for it—went like this: The customer waits awhile on hold. And when he hears me say in my brand-new accent, "Thank you for calling Handel Computer Corporation, may I please verify your name and computer model number?" he thinks: *Another goddamn foreign call center.* His expectations diminish. Rather than satisfaction, he expects courteous but ineffective service from somebody thousands of miles away. And a customer base with lowered expectations means that Handel Computers can generally avoid paying for actual tech support and replacement parts.

What Arihant has done is to implement a key cost-saving service, heretofore handled beyond our shores, right on good old American soil.

I handle thirty-seven calls today, seven above quota, before shutting off my computer terminal and heading for the parking lot. The sun has set and the evening is cool and pleasant, and for the briefest moment I feel as if I'm in the exact right spot in the universe. But as I begin to drive past residential streets and see the decorations—Santa on his sleigh, a blow-up snowman—I begin to feel nostalgic for those frigid northern winters. Unable to face my parents, I told them I had to stay here over Christmas to study.

"My son, the scholar," my old man said. "I'm sad, but impressed."

For decades, my father was an editor at the *Asbury*

Park Press but recently got laid off. Now he's writing a book about the decline of print journalism. The man writes a great sentence, but I can't imagine who would want to read about anything so obvious. It's like writing a book about the wetness of water. "How about just for a few days?" he asked.

I can live a lie over the phone and in emails. But to stay in my parents' house over the holidays would've been too much. "Wish I could, Dad," I told him.

I know they're disappointed. Driving home, I try to tell myself that I did the right thing. Then I start thinking about the doctoral student, Josephine. When she spoke about her dissertation, the phone line practically hummed with anxiety. I should have told her to take a day or two off. Drive to New Orleans and clear her head. That would have been good advice. But I'm not paid to give good advice. That's the job of the handful of actual computer techs on-staff, who handle only the most urgent problems. The rest of us, earning far less, run interference. We're polite. We ask the customer to reboot. To make sure all cables are plugged in tightly. We do our best, then we lose the call. Losing the call is pretty much the key part of my job.

Here's what I know happened the moment I hung up on Josephine: At first she wondered about the absence of hold music. Then, realizing the call had been disconnected, she became furious with me, with Handel Computers, and with the U.S. economy in general. This is the kind of service you get, she'd be thinking, when you ship all the jobs overseas. Her instinct would be to call back immediately and demand a supervisor, maybe even the head of the whole department.

All part of the plan. Because then—and here's the important part—she looked at her watch and realized that she'd just spent thirty minutes on hold (our hold music is on a 15-second loop, making even the shortest hold-time feel endless) and another thirty minutes with me, only to achieve nothing. Screw it, she eventually decided. Her time was too valuable. For now, she'd use the computer without the damn CD-ROM drive.

If she ever calls back, it'll be weeks from now, late at night, when she's unable to sleep. Might as well give it one more shot, she'll think, and get out of bed. After another thirty minutes on hold, she'll speak with another compassionate but unhelpful member of the Handel customer service team who will, as trained, lose her call again.

Nobody ever calls back a third time.

I'm halfway home when I come across a small puppy walking along the shoulder of the road. I pull over and get out of the car to investigate. The animal is young—maybe eight or nine weeks. No collar. Malnourished. People in Mississippi have different relationships with their animals than they do in New Jersey, but still. A puppy is a defenseless creature, and somebody chose to dump it here at the edge of a residential neighborhood so it would become somebody else's problem. At times like this I fear for the human race.

I kneel down. "Hi, little puppy." A puppy should be happy to see you. It should come over, tail wagging. This one glances up at me and looks away. It takes a few shaky steps in the other direction.

I scoop it up and place it on my passenger seat. A few miles away, at the vet school, is a 24-hour clinic. I could go there, but I won't. Applications were due two weeks ago, and I failed to send in mine. True, that application was my entire reason for staying in Mississippi this past year. But as the deadline neared, those 50/50 odds started to weigh on me. I couldn't stand the thought of getting rejected—or, worse—getting accepted and then flunking out again. I started thinking that when you only get accepted into one school out of twenty applications—which was what happened the first time around—maybe it means that the other nineteen schools knew what they were doing.

When I was flunking out last year, the dean called me into his office, where I flopped around like a hooked fish trying to save himself. "All I ever wanted was to be a veterinarian, sir," I told him. Just one semester living in the South and I'd already fallen into the habit of calling everybody "ma'am" and "sir." It's one of the reasons, besides the easy availability of cheap non-union labor, why Arihant set up shop here. No one needs to be taught courtesy. "Ever since I was a little kid, when my dad brought home those two baby chicks for Easter, and they got sick and died. Ever since then, I've wanted to help animals."

The dean, a round-gutted Southern gentleman who smelled of spicy cologne and horses, had a habit of sighing deeply, as if he'd just finished a big meal and now felt guilty for it.

He sighed deeply. "I've always wanted to play shortstop for the St. Louis Cardinals. Do you see what I'm saying, Charlie?"

That conversation kept weighing on me as the new deadline neared. It kept me from downloading the required forms, kept me from ordering my college transcripts and writing the entrance essay. I couldn't face the thought of another meeting with the dean. So I chickened out.

I'm not sure if it's chickening out now, too, or if it's the opposite—that maybe I'm showing resolve—but I head away from the vet school and toward home. When I arrive, I get the puppy crate out of the garage. I fostered several puppies the semester I was enrolled—lots of vet students do it—and accrued a lot of pet supplies.

I sit on the garage floor and examine the dog: short hair, big floppy ears, long tail. Probably a hound mix. She'd be cute if she weren't all ribs.

She doesn't appear to be injured—just malnourished and flea-ravaged. But my laundry room closet is filled with supplies: flea shampoo, antibiotics, pills for heartworm, tapeworm, cures for every ailment, courtesy of the vet school.

"You're gonna be okay," I tell her, running a flea brush through her matted fur. "I'm gonna make you well, little lady."

Unless she has parvo. Then she's finished.

I shouldn't have told the Easter chick story. I remember lying in bed after my meeting with Dean McKenzie—the blinds drawn, a cliché of depression—and thinking that I should have told him what mattered most, which is that when I was twelve years old, my family's Doberman Pinscher bit my friend Seth and had to be put down. It's a story I don't ever tell—I still ache over it a dozen years later—but my meeting with the dean would have been the right time. Especially since it was the truth. I believed that my becoming a vet might help to make up for getting our family dog killed.

I won't romanticize my relationship with Pongo. His bark rattled the windows. His chronic accidents on the dining room carpet put a constant scowl on my mother's face. He killed the occasional gopher or baby rabbit unwise enough to find itself in our lawn, and even though it was just the dog doing what he was hard-wired to do, the carnage always upset me.

Still. When I entered the house after school, he would follow me from room to room. He fetched a stick like it mattered, he had a belly that loved being scratched, and he was a licker, not a nipper. I taught him tricks, and my parents told me I had talent as a dog-trainer. What I had was patience, an even temper, and a smart animal. At two years old, though, the dog was still too energetic for his own good.

My friend Seth Hagerman was like an untrained dog, good-natured but mannerless. His voice was always twenty decibels too loud and he had no sense for how to respect an animal. One Saturday afternoon, my parents decided to go to a matinee and leave me at home unsupervised for a few hours—a new and wonderful development since my twelfth birthday.

Seth and I were in our small living room, sitting on the carpet in front of the sofa and watching professional wrestling on TV. During a commercial break, Seth turned to me and said, "Let's wrestle." I was never a physical kid, but Seth had three older brothers and no qualms about pinning me to the ground. I strained to get free but was too weak. Pongo watched us, lying flat on the ground and barking, and then Seth got off me and began rousing the dog into a crazy state, teasing him with a sofa cushion, putting him in a headlock. I remember watching as Seth pinned the dog, same as he'd pinned me, and held him against the carpet. He started a slow three-count. The dog squirmed and whimpered. I knew I should tell Seth to ease up, but I was his friend, not his parent, and I was still annoyed that he'd pinned me so easily. I wanted to see if the dog would fare better than I had.

Seth had just shouted "Two!" when the dog bit his face. It was only a single bite on the cheek, not an attack, but it was no warning nip, either. Pongo immediately squirmed to his feet and, knowing he'd done wrong, scurried, tail down, to the corner of the room.

Monday morning at school, Seth was peeling back the bandage to show his six stitches to anyone who'd look. I trailed him, explaining word-for-word what my parents used to explain to me when the dog was still a puppy. *You have to be gentle with him*, I told Seth. *He's only an animal. Once you rile them up like that, it's not their fault.*

The hospital was required to notify animal control. Most family dogs are given a second chance, but the breed had a bad reputation then. Nowadays it's pit bulls. Before that it was Rottweilers. Back then it was Dobermans. Bad luck for us. Worse for him.

I'm still not sure whose fault it was. It might have been the dog's. Just because they're animals doesn't mean they're blameless. But I do know this: There are certain people in the world who have a knack for keeping the peace. And those people have a responsibility. I'm one of those people. I've always been one of those people.

Caring for a sick puppy, I remember too late, is no one-person job. When I was fostering those pound puppies, I had help from my girlfriend, Linda, a fourth-year with confidence and clinical experience. We didn't date long, just a few months. When I flunked out of school, her pity seemed to loom large, and I decided I couldn't be around her or our vet school friends. The last time she and I spoke, she informed me that she was staying an extra year for her internship and offered to help me with my application this time around. That's the kind of person she is. I told her I had it all under control, even though I didn't. That's the kind of person I am.

I'd sure accept her help tonight, though. I lie on the kitchen floor next to the crate and fail to guess when the puppy will suddenly squat and pee or, worse, excrete something truly awful. The night passes glacially—the puppy whimpers, a car passes out front, the refrigerator motor clicks on, then off. Every couple of hours, I turn on the kitchen light, let the puppy out of its crate, and measure out and administer various medicines.

I begin to think, as I'm prone to do late at night, about booking a flight and traveling halfway across the globe, all the way to Veraval, India. Except for coming south to Mississippi, I haven't traveled much, haven't ever left the country other than for one drunken spring break in Cancun, which reminded me an awful lot of Wildwood, New Jersey. So I wouldn't mind seeing the Eiffel Tower, or Big Ben or whatever. But what I'd really like is to walk the beaches of Veraval. I'd like to smell the fish as they're being gutted and talk to the people who are gutting them, even if we're speaking two different languages. I'd like to visit the ancient Nawabi summer palace, which, according to Wikipedia, is mainly ruined but still standing.

At some point I notice that the sky is becoming lighter, revealing a frosty December morning. I'm sweaty with exhaustion. I take the dog outside again, then crate her, take a long shower, throw on some clean clothes, and drive to Arihant. Carrying a full-to-the-brim coffee mug, I mumble hello to some co-workers and head to my cubicle. As I plug in my headset, I'm actually looking forward to the human voices about to come through my telephone extension, even if all they're doing is complaining.

Mid-morning, a group of new hires passes by. They're practicing their new accents on one another. A middle-aged woman wearing a Rudolf the Reindeer sweater gives me a friendly wave. Rudolf's nose is a red button. I wave back.

The real city of Veraval, I learned from the internet one sleepless night, is suffering from the global recession. Fish exports are down. The cement plant is producing cement just three days a week. The rayon manufacturer is close to bankruptcy. No business has gone unaffected. Men are leaving their families to seek out work. Raj, if there really were a Raj, would most likely be in a desperate situation.

But here at Arihant we're thriving. So is our little Southern town. There used to be no bowling alley. You had to drive to Meridian for decent Chinese food.

Before Arihant, we were a one-horse town. Now we have at least three horses.

Her call comes a little past noon, the same time as yesterday. I was about to head home and let the dog out of its crate. But when I say, "Thank you for calling HCC, this is Raj speaking, may I ask for your Handel warranty code," and she says, "Is this the same Raj as yesterday?" and I say, "Josephine?" the dog slips my mind and I feel a small thrill.

"Yep," she says. "It's me."

And then I say something way out of bounds: "Buenos días, amiga."

Fortunately, her response is without suspicion. "You speak Spanish, too? My god, we Americans are provincial."

"I do not," I tell her. "Those are the only words I know. So how is your dissertation today?"

"We got cut off, you know."

"We did?"

Repeat customers are strongly discouraged. If a customer on my line tries to reconnect with Sanjay, for instance, then I'm supposed to say that Sanjay is home sick, or on vacation. If the customer is insistent, I'm supposed to say that Sanjay isn't actually at home or sick, but rather that he no longer works here. We're not supposed to say that Sanjay (or Bintu, or Leema, etc.) is deceased, but there are times when death is necessary.

What accounts for Josephine ending up on my line again? Pure chance. Her call was the next on the queue when I answered.

"When you went to transfer me," she said, "the call got screwed up. I was pretty fucking mad, pardon my French. But I feel a little calmer today."

"Yes, I deeply apologize," I tell her. At Arihant, we are always deeply apologizing. "But if you'll hold just a moment, I'll connect you now—"

"*Wait*," she says. "I mean, that'd be fine. But listen. I was wondering—what's it like in Veraval?"

Ah, I think. So you *are* lonely.

A surprising number of customers engage us in small talk. The human impulse to forge a connection runs deep. That, and the impulse to manipulate a situation—as if by getting to know us a little, we'll fast-track them toward a new computer. During orientation we were given a sheet titled *Facts About You*. I keep mine tacked to the wall of my cubicle.

> Who Do You Work For?: Never say that you work for Arihant. Instead, say that you work

> for the Handel Computer Corporation (You may also use the letters HCC).
>
> Where Are You?: Veraval, India. It is located on India's west coast.
>
> Veraval's chief industry: Fish exporting.
>
> Have You Ever Been To America? No. (Nor are you familiar with any part of American geography. If you must, say this: No, though I would like to someday. Or this: No, though my [relative] went to [name of major American university]).
>
> Your first language: Hindi. But you studied English in school from early on.
>
> Type of fish caught/processed in Veraval: Ribbon fish, cuttlefish, squid.
>
> What time is it right now where you are?: Add 10.5 hours to the current time.

I find myself giving Josephine an unusually detailed answer, telling her what I imagine to be true in my city-by-the-sea and what I imagine would be true about Raj—how he comes from a long line of fishermen, how his family and friends view him with admiration but also skepticism because of his education and indoor job. And because this life I'm describing is fantasy, I tell her that I have plans to travel to America one day to earn an advanced degree.

"Oh, you should," Josephine says. "I can tell you're ambitious. A lot more than I am, that's for sure."

"I don't understand," I say. "You are earning your doctorate."

"Yeah. About that—do you mind if I tell you something? It's kind of a confession. I wouldn't mind getting it off my chest."

The puppy has been in its crate for over four hours and needs me. I have to leave, but I can't help lowering my voice and saying, "Your confession is safe with me."

Last week, I overheard two co-workers talking at lunch about a caller who confessed to being involved in an extra-marital affair. Customer confessions aren't so rare. People need to unburden themselves, and they believe we're a world away.

I want to believe, though, that this conversation is different. Josephine's voice yesterday held a mix of desperation and camaraderie, which was why I decided to tell her my life story, fictitious as it was. Now that we've had these exchanges, isn't it at all possible that we're forming a bond, this stranger and I?

"I fabricated all my data," she says. When I don't say anything right away, she adds, "Do you know that word? Fabricated?"

I want to hear her say it again. So much so that I tell her, "No. I do not know this word."

"It means I made it all up. Five years of data. None of it's real."

"You are talking about your dissertation now?"

"Of course."

"What about your dreams of data files?" She is suddenly fascinating to me. "Are you not having those dreams?"

"Sure I am. I'm scared to death of getting caught. I've accepted a lot of grant money."

"Why did you make up your data?"

"You're a smart man, Raj. You can figure it out." Of course I can. But then she tells me anyway. "It wasn't coming out the way I wanted. This was easier. I got lazy."

"I see."

"*You see?* What are you, a therapist?"

"I mean, I get it," I tell her.

"You *get* it?" Her voice rises in pitch. "Jesus, don't you have anything to say that *means* anything?"

She's been holding her secret for so long that there's

no way for my reaction to match her expectation. "What would you like me to—"

"Well, *I* don't know," she says. "I'm an American doctoral student who just admitted to fudging all her data. Be shocked or something. Call me a bitch."

The word jolts me back to standard protocol and stilted syntax: "I am not calling you that. But if you will hold a moment—"

"Do you have a wife, Raj?"

Her question surprises me enough that I answer it truthfully.

"A girlfriend?" she asks.

"No."

"Are you gay? Do you have a homosexual lover?"

I tell her I am not homosexual.

"I'm naked, you know," she says. "I'm naked right now and touching myself."

I disconnect the call.

The puppy is worse. She has soiled her crate and barely lifts her head to look at me. She finally stands, shakily, tail drooping. I clean her with a damp towel, carry her out to the yard, and wait for her to do her business. This comes in the form of bloody diarrhea. No, not exactly. There is only blood. I run inside for a bowl of water and a can of wet puppy food. She isn't hungry or thirsty. I dip my fingers into the water and hold them up to her muzzle. She licks the water off them, but she needs more fluids. And I swear she's skinnier than yesterday.

I'm cursing myself for not getting home earlier, but the real mistake happened yesterday, when I decided to take her home and save her myself. She needs to be hydrated intravenously. Or maybe not. I'm in over my head. In fact, I know only two things for certain.

One: I've failed.

Two: The dog needs a vet.

The only animal hospital in town is fully booked for the day. There are only two vets working there, the receptionist explains, and Dr. Blinder is off buck hunting with his brothers in Missouri.

"Are you sure the other doctor can't make time?" Evidence that I'm no longer new to Mississippi: I'm unfazed by a vet who hunts.

"Sir," the receptionist says, "if it's an emergency, you should try the veterinary school."

And so I do what I must—I call Linda's cell—and when she answers we have a no-nonsense clinical conversation that ends with me carrying the puppy in its crate to the car and driving to the vet school's emergency clinic.

Linda is from New Jersey, too: Paramus. Shortly after we met, we learned that as teenagers we used to hang out at the same malls. She came to Mississippi to specialize in large animals—horses, cows—and there is something both rough and reassuring in the way she handles the puppy. Linda's hands are dry and raw from washing them all day long, but she looks pretty in her green scrubs, and I remember how she would sometimes wear a freshly laundered pair for pajamas.

She shakes her head. "We've got one sick patient on our hands."

I was right—the dog needs intravenous fluids, and I hold her still while Linda inserts the needle. This should be painful, but the dog doesn't make a sound.

"Good girl," Linda says.

While we wait for the bag of saline to drain, I ask Linda if she has nice holiday plans, and she tells me that she does. She asks me if I got my application off okay.

"It's out of my hands now," I tell her.

She inserts the IV into two other places on the dog's back, and the animal begins to look puffy from the sacs of water that have inflated under her skin.

Linda collects a fecal sample from the dog to test for parvo and heads off to the lab, which these days is off limits to me. I stand beside the examination table, pet the dog, and wait. When she returns a few minutes later, her expression reveals nothing. But when she says, "It's negative," I feel myself exhale.

"Don't feel too relieved," she quickly adds. "If she caught the virus recently, it might not show up yet on the test." She tells me to take the dog home, give her the meds, and hope for the best. "And no food," she says. "Not for a day or two."

"But she's so skinny already. . ."

When Linda looks at me, her face softens. "Look, Charlie—she's either going to perk up or she's going to get more dehydrated and die. Either way, it's going to happen fast."

"Don't you think she should stay here?"

"There's nothing we can do for her here that you can't do at home." Linda strokes the dog's head. "Trust me, she'll be better off with you." *I'm not the vet!* I think. *They kicked me out, remember?* As if reading my thoughts, she adds, "If you want, I could come by later and help out."

I can feel it again, the pity, and tell her no thanks.

We ease the dog back into her crate, and Linda jots down a medication schedule. She loads me up with cans of prescription puppy food and more drugs. I can't decide if I should give Linda a hug, or a kiss on the cheek, or maybe just a handshake. In the end, I don't touch her at all.

"Thanks," I tell her.

She smiles. "It's all right, Charlie. It's what I do."

Back at home, the call to my boss goes fine. I haven't used a single sick or vacation day since taking the job, and my complete lack of a social calendar has been misinterpreted as dedication.

I carry the crate into my bedroom, shut the blinds, turn off the light, sit on the bed, and watch the dog sleep. Were it not for this animal, I would be fielding phone calls, soothing ruffled feathers, making empty promises until five p.m., when I would go to the Tavern or maybe Big Daddy's for a burger and a few beers. I'd watch whatever game was on TV over the bar, soaking in the warmth of others' conversations, until at some point I'd feel tired and sober enough to drive home, where there is more TV and an internet that will connect me to absolutely anything, you name it, including pornography.

Some days, especially when the weather is warm and sunny, I imagine that my current life is rehabilitative. I'm off the grid, an explorer in this small town of crepe myrtles and catfish po-boys, working a secret job, almost as if I were C.I.A. I tell myself that someday I'll return to New Jersey a little worldlier than those around me, full of Southern yarns and witticisms. I'll be the life of the party.

I've been feeding this story to myself because loneliness, if you dwell on it, only gets worse. It makes a person do strange things. For instance, before I left work today, I jotted down Josephine's telephone number on a scrap of paper. And I find myself, now, taking off my shirt and pants, and then my boxer shorts, and when I'm lying completely naked on the unmade bed I use my cell phone to dial her number.

I'm wondering whether she'll pick up—she won't recognize my name on the caller ID—and what I'll say if she does. She answers on the second ring.

"Josephine?" I say. "This is Raj calling. From HCC."

"Oh," she says, her voice flat. "The caller ID said *C Falcone*."

I explain that I'm not calling from my usual extension.

"I want to apologize for hanging up on you this morning."

"Really? No, I'm the one who needs to apologize. What I said earlier. . ."

"It's okay."

"No, it isn't," she says, her voice more animated. "It's fucking crazy. I mean, who *says* that? Don't answer. I'll tell you: a fucking lunatic, that's who."

"Please. Josephine." At first, I thought the reason I was calling her had to do with sex, but now I see it's something else. "You should cut yourself some slack," I tell her, and think: *forbidden diction!* I'm still keeping up the accent, still using my invented name. I take a slow breath. And in my full-on Jersey dialect, doing my best impression of myself, I say, "Anyway, I think it's time for *me* to make a confession."

I start with my company's Big Secret. Her response—"Holy shit!"—reminds me of the older gentleman I first trained alongside. "I mean, that's so monumentally fucked up," she says.

"Agreed," I tell her.

"And evil.

"You could say that."

"I *am* saying that. And it's racist as hell," she adds.

"We're in total agreement," I tell her. "It's the fucking worst." I'm feeling a little lightheaded from saying true things over the phone.

"Then why would you work there?" she asks.

"Because they hired me," I tell her, which sounds flip but is simply more truth. And suddenly, I'm telling her about flunking out of vet school, and I tell her I've got a sick animal on my hands, and if the dog doesn't die on her own I'll probably find a way to screw up and kill her anyhow. Telling Josephine these things feels like when you've been holding your breath underwater for too long and then you surface and take that first greedy gulp of air.

The silence at the other end of the line makes me think that she's hung up the phone. But then I hear a sigh. "So 'Raj'—that's a bullshit name, right? You're 'C Falcone.'"

"Charlie," I tell her.

"You really have some accent there, Charlie," she says.

"They trained us well. There was a linguist, and—"

"I'm talking about your New Jersey accent."

"Oh." I can't help smiling. It's human nature to fantasize, and what I fantasize is that we become friends. She lives in Memphis, just a few hours away. And if she's half as lonely as I am, and especially with the holidays so close. . . . "It sounds like we both have a few secrets, don't we?"

"Yeah. Well, about that. I should probably tell you something." Now, I assume, is when she'll mention the boyfriend or the husband, and I'll be quick to assure her that it doesn't matter. This is no longer about sex, if it ever was. I'll tell her that speaking to her, like this, means a lot. It doesn't solve everything, or anything, but that doesn't make it unimportant, this unburdening—even to a stranger. "The truth," she says, "since we're being truthful—is that I lied to you. About my dissertation. It isn't fabricated. Every bit of it is legit."

This isn't the confession I expected. "For real?"

"Of course," she says.

"Then why did you. . ." But I know. It should have occurred to me that our customers' confessions might be false. That maybe they're less interested in admitting a sin than in inventing a life.

"Let's just say that writing a dissertation isn't the best thing for one's mental health," she says. "You're in your own head all day long, except for when you meet with your dissertation director and *she* tells you that your methodology is wrong. Which means another six months in this hellhole. You can't imagine the neighborhood I'm living in, because my student stipend is so laughable. I'm not talking about roaches, either—I'm talking gunfire in the middle of the day. Heavy artillery, too, if you ask my landlord—who, by the way, sold me a .38 for protection and even showed me how to use it."

As I get this glimpse into her real life, I sympathize with her—how could I not?—but I feel betrayed. Her deep, dark secret, which led me to tell her mine, has ended up being no secret at all.

"But all this is temporary," I remind her. "Your dissertation will be behind you soon."

"Sure it will," she says. "Along with the last five years of my life." She is upset suddenly, her words sounding as if they're coming through tears. "And when I'm already feeling like shit, and then I call a customer service line for help and get jerked around, and hung up on. . ."

I decide to give her some actual, practical advice. "Do you have a flash drive? You know, for backup?"

"I don't know. I think so."

"Listen to me," I say, trying to sound soothing. "I want you to back up your dissertation. I field calls all day long from customers who've had their computers crash. Trust me, the computer you bought sucks."

"Yeah, I'm pretty bad at backing things up. . .but I just found one of those thingies here in my drawer while we were talking."

"Good. Back up your dissertation."

"Okay, Charlie. Point taken. I will."

"No, I mean do it now. While I stay on the line. Otherwise, you won't—I know what people are like."

She laughs a little into the phone. "You don't mind holding?"

I tell her I'm glad to—that it will be payback for all the customers I've put on hold. She says okay and sets her phone down. It's good to feel useful. I can't fix all of her problems, but I can make sure her data doesn't get lost. And just knowing that makes me feel a little better.

While I'm waiting, I think about whether I should stay at home tomorrow, assuming the dog lives through the night, or whether I should take her with me to work. With all the medication she's on, it would be easier to take her. She'd be safe in the crate, and I'd feel better being able to look in on her—

My thoughts are interrupted by a distinct "Fuck!" This is followed seconds later by "Jesus. Oh, Jesus."

"Josephine?" I say into the phone.

The expletives—distant, as if coming from across the room—keep coming and coming. It's a little frightening, as if she's been hurt somehow—electrocuted? Did something fall on her?—but then I listen past her words to the emotion behind them, the particular mode of anger. I've heard this before. I've *sounded* like this before, working late at night on a college paper, when I'm exhausted and not thinking as clearly as I should be.

It's the sound, I realize, of losing all your data.

"Charlie!" She's back on the line now. "Jesus, Charlie, I think I did it the wrong way." She's speaking very quickly. "I think I saved the old file over the new one. Oh, shit shit shit."

"How old is the old file?"

"It's . . . I don't know. A couple of *years*! Oh, Jesus, Charlie. . ."

"What about your old computer? Didn't you just buy this one?"

"I threw it away. It's gone."

The spit has dried in my mouth. "Don't do anything," I tell her, trying to maintain a calm voice. "Don't touch anything." I wish I knew how to help her, but all my training is in avoidance. "I'm going to call work right now and get one of the real tech guys to call you right away. These guys are good, Josephine. They'll be able to help you. They're going to walk you through this."

I don't know whether this is true or not. If the file's been overwritten, it's been overwritten. Gone is gone. Or not. I just don't know.

"Charlie. Oh, fuck. Oh . . . oh. . ." the sound she starts making then isn't English. It isn't even words. It's a horrible, retching sound, and I feel desperate to make it stop.

"Are you okay?" I ask. "Please, try to relax. It's going to be all right. I promise. Please. I'll get someone to help. They'll be calling your cell in just a couple of minutes. Can you hear me? This will all be fine."

I dial the direct extension for tech support and ask for Randy Adams, the supervisor. I don't like Randy. He drives a BMW and calls everyone "big guy." Still, he's the man to call, so I call him.

He listens to my predicament and says, "The girl's probably fucked."

"Are you sure?"

"No, that's why I said probably."

This is why I try to avoid Randy Adams. "But you have to call her and try to help. Or somebody does. She's really losing it."

He yawns audibly into the phone. "All right. It probably won't be until tomorrow, though."

"No, that's no good," I explain. "I told her somebody would be calling right away."

"Now why would you do that?"

No answer would satisfy him. And anything truthful—*Because it's the right thing to do. Because she knows all our secrets*—would get me reprimanded or fired. "Randy, *please*—do me a personal favor."

"Who did you say you were again?"

I repeat my name. Then I say, "I go by Raj," and describe where my cubicle is located. "Just have someone call her as soon as you can," I say.

"As soon as I can?" He laughs. "Now *there's* a promise I can keep."

Five minutes later, my cell phone rings. It's Josephine. I don't want to answer, but I do anyway.

She's discovered language again.

"Where's the fucking tech support, Charlie? You said they'd call."

I tell her it's imminent.

"It had better be—for your sake."

"It's coming," I say. "Guaranteed."

Another ten minutes goes by and my phone rings again. I don't answer. When a message is left, I delete it without listening and call Randy again. He's out on dinner break. I ask for another tech. I'm put on hold. After the hold music loops forty or fifty times, I hang up.

Ten minutes after that, Josephine calls again.

I shut off the phone.

A magazine is glanced at and returned to the bedside table.

The ceiling is studied.

Finally, I put on the television and settle on the weather channel—but the weather channel is playing cheery Christmas songs, so I shut off the TV and stare at the bedside clock until the numbers tell me it's time to administer the antibiotic. Then more ceiling-staring until it's time for the anti-diarrhea.

At some point long after the sun goes down, I remember that I haven't had any food since breakfast.

I make a sandwich, eat the sandwich. Then back to the bedroom. I flick on the bedside lamp to look at the schedule that Linda drew up, then flick the light off again. Between the frequent administering of medications and a fruitless attempt to keep the dog's crate clean, I know I'll be awake all night. The minutes and hours creep along as I wait for the next time to give a pill or squirt medicine or remove a soiled towel from the crate. By midnight, the dog has soiled so many towels that I can't keep up with the washing and decide to use t-shirts—first the cheap white ones, then whatever I happen to grab out of my dresser in the dark.

But here's the thing: Sometime after 1 a.m. I drop into a deep sleep, and when I awake again it's to the sound of the puppy walking around in her crate.

Despite the drawn blinds, the room is beginning to lighten. I'm shocked to see it's 8:05—I never expected to sleep so soundly, and now I'm late for work. I sit up in bed and take a look. The dog is perched on my Metallica concert t-shirt, looking up at me. Tail wagging.

She isn't a new dog, but all that medicine must have kicked in overnight, and when I carry her out to the yard she actually squirms in my hands like a real live animal. I won't understate the feeling: It's magnificent. She does her business, which is noticeably less disgusting than yesterday's. It's another frosty morning, crisp, a morning with possibilities, and it occurs to me what a difference even an awful night can make.

I decide that it is most definitely take-your-puppy-to-work day.

I give her water, then take the bowl away and crate her again while I get dressed—I'm running late and skip the shower—and then carry the crate out to the car. Most of the houses on my street have their Christmas decorations up. It's the sort of neighborhood I'd never be able to afford up north. In Hoboken I paid a fortune for a one-bedroom apartment with the shower in the kitchen. Now I pay half that for a house with a dishwasher and washer/dryer, with a yard out back where this dog, should she survive, would enjoy romping.

I head to work with Josephine on my mind, my guilt diminished somewhat by my motivation to get her some much-needed help when I arrive. She almost certainly did not receive a call from tech support yesterday. Her night must have been awful. But I'm going to help her today. I'll camp out in Randy Adams's office all morning if I have to. I'll plead with my boss. I'll get it done.

I turn on my cell phone and brace myself for the voicemails, but there are none—only missed calls: seven from Josephine, all in a two-hour span last night, and two from my mother this morning. I call my mother as I drive.

"Thank God," she says. "Are you all right?"

"Relax, Mom, it's only been a couple of weeks." Actually, it's been longer than that. We don't talk nearly enough, because of the lie. It's something I need to remedy. I know that. Hearing her voice, I'm transported to frigid New Jersey. I see mulled wine on the stove and a fire in the fireplace and every other damn Christmas cliché in the book—but I also see the puppy, peeing on their kitchen floor and pulling ornaments off the tree and getting into all sorts of trouble, and I want all of it. "Anyway," I tell her, "I think I'm going to—"

"The news," she says. "Isn't that your town? I've been watching all morning."

"Isn't *what* my town?" I ask.

I round the vast magnolia trees at the entrance to Arihant to find myself facing the flashing lights of emergency vehicles. Not just a few. The parking lot has been overtaken with police cars and ambulances and firetrucks, which have created a barrier between the building and the dozens of people—my co-workers—who must have been evacuated and are now gathered in clumps along the lot's perimeter. Away from the fluorescent lights of our cubicles, these people look strange to me, alien, but as I drive closer I see it isn't the light, but rather the sagging posture and contorted faces of the grieving.

This is no fire drill, no bomb scare.

"I have to go," I tell my mother.

Only when I get out of the car do I notice the news helicopters hovering overhead. Uniformed police are everywhere. Police tape blocks all the entrances to the building. I try to imagine what must be inside: the bodies, the blood.

The dog must not like being alone in the car, because she emits a piercing cry and begins to bark. So I open the back door, get her from the crate, and approach one of the police officers, a thick man wearing sunglasses.

"What happened?" I ask, though I already know. This is the new millennium, after all, and I own a television and a computer. I read the news. My entire life, I've grown up seeing this parking lot, these first-response vehicles flashing their harsh lights. I can easily decode this message.

"Do you work here?" he asks.

I tell him I do.

"There's been gunfire reported. That's all I can say."

"Was it the tech support people?" I ask.

He looks at me and frowns. “I don’t know what you’re talking about.”

“It was a woman who did this, wasn’t it?” When he doesn’t answer right away, I say, “Listen, I think I know what happened. And why.”

“Is this a for-real claim?”

I nod.

He removes his sunglasses. “What’s your name?”

I tell him.

“Mr. Falcone, are you saying you know the perpetrator?” But the answer isn’t so simple, and when I hesitate the officer takes me by the arm. “We need to get you to a detective.”

Just then I feel a tap on my arm. Standing beside me is a young woman whose cubicle is across the office from mine. I don’t know her real or Indian name. All I know is that she always brings a mandarin orange to work, and for ten minutes every afternoon the air smells like citrus.

She looks up at me, eyes bloodshot. “Can I hug your dog?”

Her words make no sense, until I look down and notice what I’m carrying. So I hand the dog over. And what does this woman do? She hugs my dog. That’s all. Just hugs her and then, without another word, hands her back to me.

One of the cafeteria guys sees us and comes over. Big guy with a crew cut and a dirty white apron. I don’t know his name either. He doesn’t know mine.

“Man,” he says to me, “can I hug him, too?”

“Okay,” I say, and hand him the dog.

“Mr. Falcone,” says the cop, “you need to come with me now.”

I follow him away from the building, toward one of the patrol cars where a group of officers is gathered. But I don’t wait to start talking. I start saying things at a mad pace to this officer—I’m telling him about the secrets I never should have kept, and the secrets I never should have revealed—until he says to me, “Hold it a minute. I’m not the one who needs to know.”

I keep talking.

But at one point I turn around and see that more and more people have gathered where we stood—new hires, upper management, the girl from the mailroom—and they’re all waiting their turn to hug my dog, who doesn’t squirm or protest at all as she’s passed around from person to person. She lets herself be folded into each set of arms, remaining completely calm, either because she’s sick or because of the cold or the strange surroundings, or, more likely, because that’s the kind of animal she is.

The Highest Point in Delaware

Take Russell, with his rattail and booze-brain, flannel shirt reeking of cigarettes and weed. Six-one and growing, plenty strong, yet spine-sore from the old man's shove.

"All I know is, I've got one hero for a son," his father says, nose inches from Russell's chin, "and one loser. Take a wild guess which one you are, hot shot."

Russell's plan has always been the Marines, like his brother, whose stint began as two years of Southern pussy and fly fishing in the Chattahoochee. His letters to Russell were brief and unphilosophical, and sometimes came with snapshots. *Check out these fucking tits. Check out this fucking trout.* But now it's 2001 and he's in Kuwait, soon to be sent to Afghanistan. And Russell is having second thoughts.

Without a word, he leaves the kitchen. Tries to cool off with a hot shower. It's the one place where he can't hear the TV, which even on Saturday night is tuned to the 24-hour news.

After dressing again in the same jeans, same flannel shirt, same pair of boxers, he heads back downstairs and immediately fucks up again, doesn't plan on it but can't help himself, lets it slip that all he's trying to say is maybe there are better ways to live than going to the desert to get killed.

That's when his father slams him against the refrigerator and tells him he might as well assassinate his own brother, you spoiled little shit.

The marquee outside Klassy's Café hangs just low enough for pranks. And tonight there will be one, thanks to the Three Musketeers. That name, it only got uttered once, by Rhonda, the first time she got high with Russell and Mick in the woods behind Coover Lake. That was last summer, and no one's mentioned it since, because the words were embarrassing the moment they left her lips. But secretly they all liked it. Now, at 2 a.m. on a warm November night, they stumble down Route 41, guts full of Meister Bräu, heads full of weed, sky spinning like they're on a merry-go-round. They crush the last empties and kick them as they walk. They laugh about a movie no one's seen. Russell and Mick try to get Rhonda to lift her shirt and flash the drivers as they pass.

"Sorry," she says. "Not drunk enough."

Delaware is at war, and patriots are everywhere. For weeks, the high school has been holding assemblies where students come face to face with heroes. A retired Air Force pilot. A scientist. A stay-at-home mom. A firefighter who worked lower Manhattan and would've been killed with all the others had he not eaten a bad hamburger and come down with food poisoning. A man who graduated from this very high school some twenty years earlier and is climbing the highest peak on every continent. Four down, three to go.

He's also a surgeon.

"You have to believe in yourself," he says, and flashes teeth as white as his white, white shirt. "In America, you can do anything you want. Be anything you want." After this many assemblies, everyone knows when to applaud.

"Thank you," the man says. Then his smile disappears. "But that's exactly why the rest of the world is so darned jealous of us."

Two months earlier. Thursday night, late September. Mick, Russell, and Rhonda are driving to Pizza Hut, the only place open past midnight if you're underage.

"Over there!" Mick points. "There's a new one!"

Russell stops the car by the side of the road so they can all see the marquee in front of Seafood Heaven:

GOD BLESS AMERICA
HADDOCK

"At least they put the haddock second," Rhonda says from the backseat.

Signs like this are everywhere, and it has become their hobby to notice. The marquee in front of the Pizza Hut reads, "CHEESE IN CRUST! GOD BLESS AMERICA." The laundromat on Naaman's Road reads, "FOLDING SERVICES AVAILABLE. GOD BLESS AMERICA." The glass window in front of World Mart has no marquee. But painted on its floor-to-ceiling windows are the words GOD BLESS AMERICA, in red, white, and blue. Letters so large they can be seen for blocks.

"What they really mean," Rhonda said, seeing it for the first time, "is, 'White people, please don't shatter our windows.'"

World Mart has hired several young boys to ride around town on bicycles and stuff mailboxes with 25% OFF flyers. But Rhonda's mother doesn't open her mail these days, because of anthrax. All their bills are past due.

◆ ◆ ◆

During one of the assemblies, they begin to work on the "God Bless America" anagram. Rhonda's idea. First thing she figures out: "Arab" and "Arabic." But Mick says she has it wrong. "This isn't a political statement. That isn't what this is about."

"It isn't?" Rhonda is on probation for slitting the tires of every car on Peabody Street, where her ex-boyfriend lives. She's big on making statements.

"No." Then Mick grins, and says the phrase he came up with yesterday and has been waiting to tell them about. BASIC GREASE MOLD. Mick is failing three classes, including English. None of his teachers would believe he's spending his free time rearranging words to form other words.

The three of them laugh until teachers shoot them looks. Then they laugh harder. On stage, an officer from the nearby army base is explaining how the world has become small and interconnected, and if this doesn't frighten you then you simply don't get it and probably never will.

During an assembly the following week, a young female surgeon whose family fled Afghanistan when she was a young girl explains how she never would have been allowed to become a physician under the Taliban.

"Or wear this cute skirt!" she adds.

People laugh.

That night, Rhonda comes up with MAGICAL BEDSORES.

On October 7, American tomahawk cruise missiles begin to tear up Kabul and Kandahar. In the packed hallway between classes, Russell doesn't even see Rhonda walk by until she's already past him. He unfolds the piece of paper she's stuck in his shirt pocket, reads it, and falls a little in love with her.

MASSACRE OBLIGED

Yet he agrees with Mick. The prank, for it to be one, must live up to the stupidity of GOD BLESS AMERICA HADDOCK.

Only once the assemblies have died down and the three friends have tacitly decided that maybe anagrams are pretty stupid anyway, only then does Russell come across a low-enough marquee. It isn't in Wilmington, but rather ten miles north, in the wealthier Hockessin, where he buys his weed. Riding past Klassy Café at the corner of a busy intersection, he bets he can stand up on his toes and reach the letters, no problem. But it's too late. Their interest has flagged.

Then, one November night two weeks later, Russell's old man shoves Russell into the refrigerator. Russell leaves the house bruised and fuming. At the gas station, he calls Mick and Rhonda. "We need to get stoned," he says, and they want to, except nobody's got anything to get stoned on. So they meet up in the parking lot of PriceRight Liquors, where luck comes their way in the form of a gray-bearded drunk, loitering by the phone booth and singing "Proud Mary." He accepts their cash in exchange for a twelve-pack of Meister Bräu even though Russell told him Bud, specifically, because that's what his brother drinks, always, even in Kuwait.

The three of them get in Russell's car, and Russell drives them to Hockessin. By the time they've drunk a couple beers apiece and are smoking up peacefully in the day-school's quiet playground, it is after midnight and the town is shut down for the evening.

Two hours later, rocking slowly on a swing, Russell has his flash of insight. Doesn't even need paper to figure it out, though he writes it with a stick in the dirt just to be sure.

"You just might be a genius," Mick says.

"I just might," Russell says.

Rhonda might have agreed, but she's too busy trying not to snarf her beer.

◆ ◆ ◆

Sixteen months later, Freedom Fries will be a hot seller in the school cafeteria. Soon after, American tomahawk cruise missiles will begin to tear up Baghdad, resulting in more assemblies. Rhonda, then a high school junior, will endure them alone. Russell will change oil at the Jiffy Lube on Route 1 during the day and look at internet porn at night. Letters from his brother will be short, infrequent, and tit-less. Mick will park cars at Bally's in Atlantic City and keep his money in a sock drawer. He'll believe that with a big enough stake, he can make a living at poker.

In a year, they'll all miss having been part of the Three Musketeers, though they won't think about it often, and never by that name.

Klassy's Café is closed, the parking lot empty, the marquee a simple GOD BLESS AMERICA. Russell hopes he is tall enough. He is. He has grown two inches this year.

When he is done making the anagram, there are two letters left over: "C" and "A." Mick throws the "C" into the woods behind the café. Rhonda takes the "A" from Mick and presents it to Russell. "I thought you should finally get one of these before leaving high school," she says, smirking.

Russell takes the letter from her. "You're a real comedian," he says, though he's touched by the gesture. For a moment he stands there watching her, seeing her under the yellow light of the marquee as even she has no idea she is capable of being seen. She tilts her head, and the only word he can think of is *angelic*.

"What's on your mind, stud?" she says, and the moment is over. He flings the letter into the woods.

"I wonder where the highest point in Delaware is?" Rhonda asks, back at the playground. It is nearly 3 a.m. They're sitting on the merry-go-round, which spins slowly under the power of their tired feet. They smoke a bowl. It isn't even cold outside. Spring has sprung in late autumn.

"We could be sitting right on it," Russell says.

"God, I hope not," she says.

But Russell believes that this must be the highest point. This, he feels damn certain, is as good as it gets.

Mick holds his lighter up to the bowl they've been passing, and inhales. Leans back, looks up at the sky, and slowly pushes the smoke from his lungs.

"It's me," he says, and coughs. "Right now, nothing in Delaware is higher than me."

They doze for an hour in Russell's car and then he drives them back to the liquor store. In the parking lot, he tries again to get Rhonda to flash the passing cars. He imagines writing about it to his brother, if she does it. He might write it anyway, even if she doesn't.

She reaches out and flicks his rattail. "Why don't you take out your little pecker and show it around instead?"

This he does.

"I'm going home," Rhonda says. "Good night, boys."

"You can't leave now," Russell says. "Not alone. It isn't safe."

"Zip up your pants and tell me that again," she says, and waves tootles, and walks to her car at the other end of the lot. "See you in church!" she says. The smack of her heavy shoes will stay with them.

A dog barks somewhere far off.

Streetlights and nearby malls and car dealerships hide the stars and tint the sky a sickly brownish-orange.

November 3, 2001. A warm evening.

Russell sleeps in his car for another hour and then drives home. He hits the bed just as the birds start and is asleep before the room begins to lighten. Almost immediately, he's awakened by his father's voice. The bedroom light is on.

"You just don't get it, do you?"

Russell's head feels sliced in half. He cracks open his eyes and makes out the shapes of his father and mother standing just inside the doorway. They're in their robes, looking old and small, and Russell wonders where the old man's strength came from earlier tonight.

"We've been attacked, son." His father's voice is high and pleading. "We're talking war. Don't you watch TV? Haven't you heard?"

"Your brother needs all of our support," his mother says. "Why is that so hard for you to understand?"

Soon, Russell will need to decide whether to join the Marines or whether to stay in Wilmington and get some shit job. It will come down, he'll eventually decide, to where he thinks he can do the least harm. But that's for later. This morning, he rolls over in his bed, away from his parents, and faces the window.

It's almost morning. He imagines the good citizens of Delaware shutting off their alarm clocks and dressing for work, getting in their cars and driving past reminder after reminder of just how much God blesses America. But some of them will see this other message, too, the new one left by Russell and Mick and Rhonda on the marquee outside Klassy's Café. The one advertising EDIBLE ORGASMS.

And isn't this, too, something they can all believe in? Something to rally behind in this dawning age of vigilance and valor?

A Vanishing Story

Dr. Allan Hunt, associate professor of linguistics and narratology at the state's leading research institution, was looking out the window of the department's third-story suite, chewing on his pencil despite writing, always, on a computer—even notes; even brainstorms; even the idlest of observations—when, absently, he reached down for his book on Mikhail Bakhtin's theory of dialogics and noticed his briefcase missing.

He remembered carrying the briefcase from the car to the student union, remembered carrying it in one hand, Starbucks cup in the other, to Bryant Hall, where he'd set the briefcase on the floor beside his office desk, same as every day, or at least he *believed* he recalled setting it down on the floor, because its absence, he fully admitted, suggested otherwise.

The most valuable loss, if the briefcase were truly gone, was the briefcase itself—a Milano Napa, black leather

(Venice collection), a gift from Gloria for his birthday, she claimed, though they both knew it was a gift of apology, a gift of *Let's give this marriage one more chance*, a gift of *See how I can pretend to respect your work?*

He was thinking, not for the first time, about the subtler meaning of the obscenely expensive briefcase, and how demeaning a gift it truly was, considering that a professor could never buy such an extravagance on his salary alone, when he heard outside his office the rhythmic *thuck thuck thuck* of the photocopy machine, and left his office to look there.

The undergraduate work study student, Jenny (or Joanie? Ginny?) looked up from the copy machine and said, "Hey, Professor Hunt," smiling, and then her smile faded, and Dr. Hunt knew she saw his pain, even if she lacked the specifics: that the divorce papers had arrived yesterday morning by courier, that his ten-year marriage was now and forever over. It made one absentminded, a marriage in its curtain-call stage, transforming otherwise articulate men into bumblers, into losers of briefcases, and he felt a fierce, momentary ache for his days as a graduate student when the particularities of language had seemed as urgent and awesome as the cosmos, that time before meeting Gloria the Great, Gloria the Gorgeous.

Yes, this girl Jenny (briefcase thief?) saw through him despite the earnest attention he'd paid to making today the start of the rest of his life—though not teaching today, he wore a sharp blazer, necktie, freshly ironed slacks, and polished shoes; he vowed to glue himself to his chair and write the article coming due next week. And as if more evidence were needed that he wasn't, perhaps, operating at full speed despite his professional attire, caffeine intake, and pledge to stop mourning his dead marriage and, instead, to focus and double-down on his scholarship, his career, his supposed lifelong passion, the girl glanced down, then up, and said, "Where's your shoe, professor?"

"How odd," Dr. Hunt muttered, seeing the black sock covering his foot, size 8-narrow, and he returned to his desk where the shoe must have come off while his mind was on Mikhail Bakhtin's notion of unfinalizability—the ultimate unknowability of another—and how, for the first time, he thought: Bakhtin, you've got it dead wrong. Because you *could* know another, and, no, people *didn't* change, not fundamentally, a lesson the professor learned not from any revered philosopher or theorist but from his wife, now his ex, who had taught him that once an adulteress always an adulteress (and, he had to admit, once a blind cuckold, always a blind cuckold).

He wondered, in a burst of bitter humor, if the ex in question was behind the disappearance of his briefcase and his shoe, just as she'd already been responsible for the disappearance of his pride and his ability to sit at his computer and finish any of the papers and articles whose deadlines loomed. Worse, yesterday afternoon he had stood in front of thirty groggy undergraduates, their notebooks and pens more stage props than learning aids, and while lecturing about essential tropes and archetypes in folktales and fairy tales, twice—twice!—the word "wolf" had come out of his mouth as "wife," as in "*the big, bad wife.*"

She had meant everything to him in part because she'd been everything: a magician, for starters, headline performer at the annual magician conventions, the Society of American Magicians and International Brotherhood of Magicians—known, especially, for her dogged resistance to cliché: forget the top-hat, the vaudeville shtick with its tired patter. A top female closeup conjurer, she nonetheless decided at age thirty, let's try medical school, and suddenly she'd aced the MCAT, and, four years later, had landed a coveted residency in radiation oncology, so now instead of making white doves disappear she had her sights on grander vanishings: carcinomas, lymphomas, astrocytomas.

"Gloria, you have broken my heart and stolen my sole," Dr. Hunt said now, and smiled, because while a bad pun was the lowest form of humor (said dramatist Allan Dennis ages ago), a good pun, Dr. Hunt believed, was an unexpected treat—a lagniappe—even for a jaded linguist.

The misplaced shoe couldn't have gone far, but it wasn't under his desk or by his computer or his bookshelf or behind the mini fridge, and he curled his hands into fists, frustrated that his mind wouldn't let his mind focus on his work, which he'd vowed to do. He needed the books in his briefcase; he needed the shoe; he needed, more broadly, to get a grip: Gloria was gone, pal, and quite likely in bed with Jack Morrow *right now*, and you—yes, you—drove her to him with your insufferable insecurities and self-pity.

No, people didn't change: just weeks after meeting Gloria, she had mentioned a second guy, nothing serious, she assured him, but rather than play it cool, Allan Hunt (not *Dr.* Hunt yet, with his dissertation ahead) had stormed off and ignored her calls for an agonizing month. Fast-forward twelve years, and we have our credentialed and respected doctor of philosophy (tenured, no less), foolish but no fool, who knew damn well he had, once again, contributed in no small way to this parting, except now it was final and exponentially more devastating.

He remembered, several months back, her sobbing to him, "You have taken me from me," and though he'd feigned ignorance, he knew what she meant: he'd grown weary of hearing about her Good Work, the lives saved, the families who'd forever be in her debt. He'd become exhausted, too, of her tales of those she couldn't help, the tragedies, the losses filling her with quiet grief, and it didn't take a scholar to read the subtext: I'm the real doctor, whose hands can heal; you, Allan, play with words. So he shut her down, shut her out, and tried to banish from their conversations even the memories of her first career, the magic shows where adoring eyes were, let's be honest already, leering eyes, and hadn't she just loved all that attention?

He was a hypocrite, though, and knew it, because part of his own love for her was in the leering, for Gloria was a beautiful creature—this woman who had chosen to stand with him before a judge and say, "I do." And they *had*, for a while, loved and honored one another, good times and bad, though he never imagined the bad would ever get as bad as Jack Morrow, radiologist with the perpetual tan, the athletic grace, the condo in Cabo. And although Dr. Hunt had written an entire dissertation on humanity's essential mutability, it was his marriage with Gloria that proved to him he had been fundamentally wrong: no, we don't change; we are always ourselves—cheater, sucker, magician, stooge.

"You've always tried to reduce me to nothing," he had told her near the end, when their home was nothing but separate beds and clanking dishes, and then he added, "but I know you're not that good a magician."

His sheer meanness initially struck her dumb, though then she sputtered, "You don't know that," and he, ignorant fool, had merely shaken his head and laughed, feeling that finally she was the one flailing and grasping for dignity. For dignity was that essential quality she'd robbed him of, bit by bit, over many years—she'd stolen his dignity the way you would rob a bank or an art museum: with patience and planning and precision. And now she was gone—like his briefcase, like his shoe—leaving him the Toyota Camry, their too-large bed (no, not too large: perfect!), his reappraisal of Bakhtin, and where the hell was his sock?

He often misplaced them at home, yanking them from his sweaty feet, but to have removed a sock at work, in his departmental office, without knowing . . . he breathed in, counted to five, and slowly exhaled. But when he reached up to run a hand through his hair, which, for a man of his age, was especially thick—his finest attribute—he gasped, because he felt no hair at all. Lowering his arm, he saw the trouble wasn't in fact his hair, but that the arm—inside his shirt, inside his blazer—ended at the wrist, and gone were the fingers and palm.

There was some blood at the wrist, which easily could be blotted, as if the surgery had gone well but required a bit of post-op attention, and Dr. Hunt cried out. That is, he tried to, only there was no sound at all, and with horror he knew the reason had to be one or the other: no mouth, or no ears.

Or both, he realized as he shot up from his chair and bolted out his office door, one shoe on, one shoe off, shouting in utter silence: *help me, please!*

Friday afternoons were always quiet on campus (even the copy machine was now abandoned), and no one saw him drop to the carpet, his other shoe gone, sock, foot. He sat and stared at his ankle as the pants faded away and the sock turned to dust and the ankle dissolved, leaving a calf with flapping skin. Then the other ankle; then wrists to the elbows, then knees, thighs, and if Dr. Hunt had lips and a tongue and a throat he would've screamed. And lungs: he needed lungs for screaming, and for breathing—and oh, God, he couldn't draw a breath, and then his vision vanished with his eyes.

His heart, though: it beat and beat and beat while his shoulders and pelvis and eyebrows and spleen and intestines all dissolved away to nothing. His nose and his liver; his ribs; his kidney; his bladder; his teeth; his veins and arteries; the muscles in his torso; his stomach. There was no pain, not a twinge, and his heart beat on, and understanding narrative, he knew he was nearing his own denouement.

He lay on the carpet by the hallway, just a heart and a brain and the rapidly diminishing viscera connecting the two. His remaining muscles caused him to turn slightly, and then those final muscles gave out and his stillness was almost complete. Electrical impulses lingered, as with a lobster sliced in half, and he barely twitched, his heart still beating, but fainter. His brain, though: it screamed on, aware of the crime against him, aware of its perpetrator, aware, aware, aware.

I am sorry I am sorry I am sorry I am sorry I am sorry I am sorry.

Any thought or feeling or reaction after that could no longer be attributed to Dr. Allan Hunt. His heart reduced to one chamber, his brain to ten million neurons, then five, then two. Then came the final reduction: shrinking, fading, desiccating, everything opaque becoming translucent and then transparent. That was how he ended, as ever-diminishing ectoplasm, no mind, no body even. A million remaining cells now one hundred thousand, now eight hundred, now fifty.

His blazer and shirt and pants, shoes and socks, skin, all gone. Organs and blood, reduced beyond the cell, to molecules, atoms, quarks. Then: particles yet to be discovered, and then smaller still. Everything he'd ever been, everything he would ever be. All of it, gone—except for his briefcase.

The Starbucks employees are keeping it safe. They figure he'll be back soon. It's awful, losing something important. He'll be so relieved.

He'll say thanks.

You're welcome.

Bye.

Mediation

When Sandy Stoddard returned home from the video rental store, there was a message from Len Brice asking her to call him at work. "It's kind of important," he said. Len worked for Sandy's husband. But William was in D.C. on business until tomorrow afternoon, and Len knew it.

She'd been having a fine day, having finished work early enough to read a newspaper over a leisurely lunch at a local Italian restaurant. Now, content from the meal and the wine that'd gone with it, she didn't feel like calling Len. Not at all. She'd call him anyway, though, believing that it was better to settle small matters before they became big ones—a belief, after all, that was at the heart of her job as mediator. Companies hired Sandy when they were being accused of wrongful termination, discrimination, or harassment. The idea was to resolve such matters quickly, before they became full-blown lawsuits that dragged on and the only winners were the lawyers.

Sandy listened to the message a second time, jotted down Len's direct line, then deleted the message.

Len answered on the first ring.

"Thanks so much for calling me back." His voice lowered. "Hang on one sec, will you?" She imagined him shutting the door to his office. "Listen"—his voice was still low—"we need to talk."

"Well, we're talking," she said, trying to sound friendly and direct. "What's on your mind?"

"No, I mean, I need to see you. This thing I need to talk to you about, I need to do it in person."

They hadn't seen each other in person, just the two of them, for years. "I'm not sure that's the best idea," she said. "Actually, I'm sure it isn't."

Two seconds on the phone, and she had it figured out: Len was going to confess his love. He was newly married. He and his wife had probably had their first fight, and he was feeling depressed and desperate. And desperate people acted desperately. It was why employees, feeling wronged, always threatened to call their attorneys, even though they almost never had attorneys.

She saw it clearly. Desperate Len grabbing for the phone, dialing up Sandy, leaving his kind-of-important message. Never mind that the entirety of their relationship these past ten years consisted of insipid hellos and how-are-yous at company parties and picnics. Standing around the keg while doughy office workers swung a softball bat and missed fly balls. But to some men, it seemed, an ex-lover was always a potential lover.

"Please," he was saying, "let me drop by the house after work."

"The house? No."

Her session at the Wonder Bread headquarters had gone well this morning—lawsuit averted, employee rehired under a new manager in a different department—

and to reward herself, on the way home she'd stopped and rented a couple of movies that William would have no interest in watching. She had been looking forward to cooking dinner and planting herself in front of the TV for the night.

"Well, then *some*where," he said.

"Somewhere else," she said. "Somewhere public."

"All right," he said. "How about the library?"

The Library was the name of a frat-boy bar near the Ohio State campus. She hadn't been there for years, not since her early twenties. She remembered sticky floors and bodies crammed together, everyone shouting at once.

"Maybe somewhere a little quieter," she said. "The R-Bar maybe? In Clintonville?"

"Quieter than . . . no, I mean the actual library. The public library downtown. At the coffee shop there."

"Oh," she said. "Okay, I can meet you there."

"No, I'm all through with bars," he said.

Strange. The Len she knew wasn't remotely through with them.

Sandy arrived first. The library was quiet, the after-school crowd having left for dinner. In the café there was just one other woman about Sandy's age. A mug sat on her table, and she looked engrossed in a paperback novel. It'd been years since Sandy had been to a library or read a book for fun.

Not that she didn't read. The books in her home office were divided into two categories. One category was comprised of the truly useful: books she'd acquired over the years on human resource management, micro-economics, leadership theory, and business law.

Then there were the other books. The pop-psychology books masquerading as business texts, written on an eighth-grade level, the ones that middle-managers devoured on trains and planes in hopes of learning the secret to wealth and power. Books that made them all talk of "being on the bus" or "seeing twenty-twenty" or whatever this month's slogan of corporate self-actualization happened to be. She despised these books for inhibiting, rather than fostering, actual thought. But she needed to be familiar with them, because so many of her clients spoke their strange language.

She ordered a cup of tea and decided that she'd like to read a novel. Before leaving the library, she'd check one out and then begin reading it in bed tonight after watching one of the rental movies.

As soon as she sat down at a table with her tea, Len came into the café wearing a rumpled gray suit. Seeing her, he smiled, and waved, and then, as if he didn't know what to do with his hand, he ran it through his graying, gel-slathered hair.

He didn't look so good anymore. That made it easier. Len was exactly her husband's age, forty. He used to look the younger of the two, and was very handsome. But while William now looked healthy and strong, entering middle age with just enough graying at the temples to make him seem worldly, Len, once full of youthful glow, even charm, had over the years become unattractive. His skin was blotchy, and he'd gained weight in the middle.

The key to handling this matter with Len, she'd decided, was to be direct and unambiguous. *There's no chance for us,* she would say. And if he asked for an explanation, she'd say, *Because I'm happily married.*

Before leaving the house, she had called William in D.C. He was between meetings. She told him briefly about the Wonder Bread account. About lunch. And as they spoke, she found herself paying attention to their easy banter, their obvious regard for each other, and she had been amused and heartened. It hadn't always been that way—there had been times when she thought it would never be that way.

Len came over to the table carrying an enormous coffee mug and sat directly beneath a poster of a hotdog wearing a gold medal. The poster said, "Reading is for top dogs!"

Len took a sip of coffee. "I didn't know if William told you about my joining A.A.," he said, and set the coffee down on the table. "I'm a caffeine man now." He flashed a mouthful of yellowing teeth.

So I have it wrong, she thought. This wasn't about the two of them after all. It wasn't about love, or sex. This was all about Leonard Brice, the Man-on-the-Road-to-Recovery.

Let the selfishness begin, she thought.

"No, he hasn't told me anything," she said. It was true. William never spoke about his A.A. meetings, or whom he saw there. And she knew better than to ask.

"Tina sort of gave me an ultimatum, before we got married."

The wedding, six months earlier, had been a simple, families-only deal. Sandy was glad. She wouldn't have wanted to attend the wedding at all, but there'd have been no avoiding it.

"Do I want to know the details?" she asked.

He smiled. "It's kind of funny, now. I'd done so many dumb things while drinking. I mean really stupid things." He sipped his coffee and waited a second. "But what put Tina over the edge was. . .well, she'd asked me to pick up her wedding dress from the alterations place because it was near my office. So I did, after hitting a couple of bars first. Anyway, the bottom of the dress got shut in the car door and I didn't notice. It was raining outside, and muddy." He shook his head. "When she saw it, she said she never saw such an obvious sign in all her life. Well, she had a point. Even I could see that."

He told it as if he'd told it before. The anecdote was too perfect, even a little charming, and almost certainly not true. She'd known some heavy drinkers over the years, enough to know that real stories of hitting rock bottom were messier than that, and usually disgusting. She hoped for his sake he was being more honest at his A.A. meetings.

"So how's that going?" she asked.

"Hands down, hardest thing I ever had to do." He folded his hands and looked at her nervously.

Before leaving the house she'd put on a darker shade of lipstick. A little extra mascara. Even though she'd anticipated rejecting Len's advances, she wanted to look good doing it. Clearly, she had the agenda wrong.

"So Len," she said, sitting up a little straighter, back in mediator mode, "why don't you tell me why you called earlier."

"All right," he said, and took a breath. "I'm going to be straight with you."

"Good. I like that."

"Okay. Here goes." He leaned in conspiratorially. "William's my sponsor."

"Well, good for you," she said, flashing a friendly smile. Was that all? It was hardly a surprise. For ten years, William had been going to those meetings. Even now, he rarely skipped more than two or three days. "He's an old pro by now. I'll bet he's a good sponsor."

"He is. I really owe him a lot. I'll tell you, those twelve steps aren't easy."

She expected him to say more, but he stopped talking suddenly, his gaze still on her. She looked up at the wiener poster, then back at Len, who was watching her closely. "No," she said, "I'd imagine they aren't."

"Especially apologizing to people. Admitting my sins to all the people I've wronged. That's one of the hardest parts about it. . ." He stopped again, as if waiting for her to piece something together. Waiting for it to click. Why the phone call. Why this meeting.

Her eyes widened. "No way." She shook her head. "Forget it. You can't tell him."

"I've wronged him, Sandy." His voice raised in pitch. "We did a terrible thing, you and I."

"Fuck you." The barista behind the counter glared at her. She looked like a librarian herself, hair pulled back, big glasses. The woman at the other table glanced up, then hid her head again behind the book she was supposedly reading. "You need to think about other people," Sandy said.

"I need to confess my sins."

"No, you don't. You need to do what's right. And what's right is to leave William alone. Our marriage is good now."

"If it's really that good, then it'll survive the truth."

"So now you're an expert on marriage?"

Their voices were too loud for a library. She felt sets of eyes peeping from around corners and between stacks of books, as if their affair were happening right now, rather than in the distant past.

"All I know is," Len said, "I've worked with William every day for ten years. Your husband is one of the finest men I've ever known. He's forgiving. It's in his nature. He'll forgive us."

"And if he doesn't?"

"Then I'll feel terrible. And most likely I'll be out of a job *and* a sponsor." He put his head in his hands. "This is why doing bad things is bad, Sandy. Because there are consequences."

His saggy eyelids, his bulbous nose. The changes had been gradual, but looking at him now, she could barely see a trace of the younger man from whom this one had emerged.

"You're talking about ancient history," she said. "It has nothing to do with us anymore. Nothing good can come from bringing it up."

He sighed deeply, as if Sandy were well meaning but slow-witted. "A recovering alcoholic needs to confess his sins and make amends to all the people he's harmed, no matter how difficult it might be. It's an essential part of the recovery process."

She slammed her hand on the table, nearly spilling their drinks. "I hate what A.A. does to all you men," she said. "It makes you selfish and takes away your goddamn common sense."

At the word "goddamn," Len flinched.

"What? What? Oh, for Christ's sake," she said, "that, too?"

She stood up, and was about to walk away from sober, God-fearing Len, newest of the Boy Scouts, when he said, "Sandy, please." She glared at him. "This is hard for me, too," he said. "William is my colleague and my friend."

"I know, Len." She was already bored with him. "And he's my husband. So it's a little harder for me, okay?" Any remaining shred of professional dispassion was gone from her voice.

"I guess you're right. But when he comes back from Washington, I'm going to tell him."

"Oh, you are, are you?"

"I'm sorry, Sandy, but that's how it has to be."

In mediator terms, this was a "no-yield statement." Hearing it, Sandy saw no reason to linger. Without another word, she walked out of the library and drove home, which she immediately realized was exactly the wrong place to go, goddamn alcohol-free zone that it was.

She'd fallen for him quickly, almost immediately, on the freezing January night of her twenty-third birthday. At the Irish pub where she'd come with her friends, he walked over and introduced himself as the "charming but sleazy salesman-type." He bought her a drink. Hours later, her friends having left ("Are you *sure* you're okay, Sandy? Are you *sure* you don't want us to get you home?"), she agreed to let this stranger named Bill walk her to her apartment.

This wasn't something she did often. Or ever.

"Cross my heart," he'd said as they were leaving the bar. "No funny business." He actually crossed his heart.

She didn't believe him, but neither did she care. She'd had exactly three lovers in her life. Each relationship had begun in friendship. Each had been slow to transition into romance, had lasted about a year, and had ended when the guy cheated on her. So why not break the pattern with a one-night stand?

"Let's get out of here," she said.

His arm around her, they stumbled down a narrow path of shoveled sidewalk that cut through the foot of snow that had fallen the previous day.

Sandy's apartment building sat up on a hilltop. At the bottom of the hill, by the dumpsters, lay a big cardboard box. It must have been left there recently, because it was nearly dry.

"We'll need this," Bill decided, and began to drag it up the hill. "And some large trash bags. Have any?"

Inside, they collapsed the box and duct-taped several trash bags to it, then went back outside and rode their improvised sled down the hill—it didn't work very well, but that didn't stop them—until, twenty or thirty minutes later, a police car came quietly to a stop at the bottom of the hill. Sandy and Bill walked over to the car.

"We've gotten a few noise complaints," the officer said though his open window.

They were being loud—laughing, carrying on. Wrestling a little in the snow. They were both very drunk.

"It's pretty late," the officer said, and raised his eyebrows. "You two probably want to think about calling it a night."

"We will, officer," Sandy said, realizing only now how cold her extremities were. She shivered, and Bill put his arm around her.

They went inside, shed coats and gloves and shoes and socks, and Sandy poured them a nightcap—small glasses of Scotch. Sandy lay on the sofa, her bare feet on Bill's lap. He rubbed her feet until they got tingly and warm.

"So you can kiss me if you'd like," Sandy said. Bill set his glass on the coffee table. He leaned down and kissed the top of Sandy's foot. "Funny man," she said.

He kissed her for real. A good, long kiss.

Then he smiled. Not the magazine-ready grin of a

sleazy-salesman type, but rather a flash of happiness and surprise. An unrehearsed smile.

Sandy lay back down on the sofa. "That was nice," she said, not sure if she meant the kiss or the smile. Not caring. Thinking only: *So this is what a spark is.*

When their drinks were done, they went into the bedroom, where Sandy put on a Cowboy Junkies CD that seemed like an appropriate soundtrack to their evening, which felt both sexy and cozy. They spoke softly under the covers until they were both sleeping. Several hours later, she woke up thirsty, the CD still repeating. She shut the music off, set a fresh glass of water on her night table, climbed back in bed, moved closer to Bill, and tapped him on the shoulder. And when he stirred, she whispered into his ear: "I really really really want some funny business."

So what's he like? her girlfriends wanted to know.

And she'd answer: *He's fun.*

That simple word fit him best. Plenty of people tried to have fun, but Bill *was* fun. And when you're with a fun man, Sandy was quick to learn, you want to keep on being with him. Sandy had graduated the year before with her sociology degree from Ohio State and was working in the human resources department of a law firm downtown. Bill worked on promotional campaigns for a bank's credit card division. These were not exciting jobs, but neither of them cared. Their work seemed secondary to the fact that life was short, that most people were unhappy, and that it was better to enjoy being young and healthy and in love while you could, than to live solely for some future that no one could predict.

They worked hard, but not overly so. They had plenty of time for each other. Plenty of time for going out, staying in, having fun. Being fun.

Within the year, they were married.

Several months later, on a drizzly April afternoon

when Bill told her he'd gone to an A.A. meeting, just to see what it was like, Sandy had been floored.

"Do you really think you're an alcoholic?" she'd asked him.

"Come on, Sandy. You know I am."

But she didn't. He didn't seem to drink any more than many of her college friends. She herself could keep up with him most nights. And he never embarrassed himself. Or at least not any worse than other heavy or even moderate drinkers she'd known.

The next day, he went to another meeting. And the day after that.

She was worried about him, and worried about them, too. She loved him exactly as he was. Neither of them wanted children. Their own childhoods had been traumatic, their genes not so wonderful that they required passing along. And anyway, the world was already overpopulated. And so theirs would be a family of two, till death do they part. So how big a change, exactly, were we talking about?

Yet this question was selfish, and she tried to push it out of the way. If he wanted to give up drinking, then of course she'd support him. She was his wife, after all.

Then God came into the picture. Suddenly there was talk of the "higher power" that William had turned his life over to. How he—and Sandy, too—were but humble servants. He spoke of taking a "moral inventory."

And then one day he asked that she start calling him William. This, after nearly two years of calling him nothing but Bill.

"But I think of you as Bill," she said. "That's who you are to me."

"Bill was a drinker, Sandy," he said. "William is a sober man, with God's help."

And overnight, it seemed, this exciting, fun man became someone who spoke in platitudes, someone whose sense of humor had evaporated, and with it his easy laugh and unrehearsed smile. And his secret attendance at these daily meetings came hand-in-hand with a secret of Sandy's own. Recovering-alcoholic William was about the dullest man she'd ever met.

She tried to tell herself that this was only a phase. She'd had friends who'd taken up dieting, say, or yoga, and become temporarily obsessed with carbs and points, with flexibility and alignment. But in time, these obsessions eased, and the person began to think and talk about other things again.

As the weeks passed, however, and the attention that Bill—William—paid to his own recovery showed no sign of letting up, she found herself more and more infuriated by this man she'd married. How serious and predictable he'd become—even in bed. Their best sex had always involved alcohol. Sober, he was inhibited and mechanical, as if making love to her was a chore that he happened to get a smidgen of enjoyment out of, like folding hot laundry.

She could hardly stand the thought of spending the rest of her life with him. Yet how could she explain to anyone, especially her husband, that she preferred him as an alcoholic? She couldn't. She shouldn't even be thinking this, let alone saying it. So she said nothing.

And when he announced one night at their favorite restaurant that he'd been sober for exactly six months, she made a show of how proud of him she was. She came around to his side of the table and hugged him. They ate shrimp cocktails and toasted sparkling waters and fell asleep that night watching Letterman.

The next day, at his company's Labor Day picnic, William left early for an A.A. meeting. Len Brice, a nice-looking man who worked in business loans, said he'd give her a lift home. This he did, though not before screwing her extraordinarily well in the backseat of his Mustang.

Early in her career, Sandy mediated a case where a sunscreen manufacturer was making a television commercial. They'd originally cast the same actress as in their prior commercials, but changed their mind at the last minute. The actress in the ad was to appear in a bikini, and the problem was that she'd gained nearly forty pounds since taping the last commercial.

She had no long-term contract with the company. They didn't owe her a reason, and they didn't give her one. Nevertheless, she had filed lawsuits against the manufacturer and the agency producing its commercials. In the conference room of a downtown hotel—neutral territory—sat Sandy, the actress, her lawyer, and representatives from the two companies. Sandy's goal walking into the room was to send the actress home with ten or twenty thousand dollars and the misconception that her weight gain was irrelevant to the companies' change in casting.

"Please," the girl had said, once all the men in the room had spoken evasively about *contractual rights*, about their ad campaign's *new direction*. She wore a navy business suit. She was very pretty, Sandy thought, though not thin. "Tell me the truth. That's all I want."

At first, Sandy had thought: how frank. How unusual.

The girl had no case. But nobody wanted the bad press, and Sandy's mission was clear. Get the girl to drop the lawsuit. Send her home with a check and a misconception.

This took less than an hour.

"Thank you," she'd said to Sandy as they walked out of the conference room together. Her eyes were wet with emotion. "Thank you for your honesty."

The girl had been wrong, Sandy realized. She hadn't wanted the truth. She wanted these people around the table to lie again, to lie better, until the lie began to feel like truth.

And this need to be lied to, Sandy found, wasn't limited to this one girl. Again and again Sandy came up against people who sued their former employers not because they'd been lied to, but because they'd finally run up against a dose of honesty. Fire somebody because "the ninety-day probationary period is in effect, and no reason is necessary," and the employee goes away and leaves you alone. But fire somebody because she's too incompetent, or too rude, or too fat for the new bikini ad, and you're asking for trouble.

If you're the employer, you become self-righteous, wondering how these people ever get the nerve, and you ask your lawyers what it'll cost to see the case through to trial. And then if you're smart you call in Sandy Stoddard, corporate mediator, to apply the salve of undeserved self-esteem and make the problem go away.

Over time, Sandy's job made her extremely practical. Or maybe it was her practicality that had led her to this career. Either way, she knew she wasn't like most people, who believed they valued absolute honesty without ever really giving the concept any thought. After ending her brief affair with Len Brice, she knew she'd never tell her husband about it. Would never tell him that she'd needed some exciting sex for a change—needed to let loose, to drink, to fuck, to give herself over to this final fling, or celebration, or mourning, or whatever the hell it was—before quietly committing the rest of her life to him.

In the years that followed, she never regretted keeping the affair from him. Not that she didn't fault herself daily while it was going on. Once, ironing a shirt of William's, she had purposely pressed the hot iron to her palm. That day the guilt had been almost too much. There had been other days almost as bad. However, once she'd broken it off with Len, she felt no compulsion to tell William about it. The affair was the transgression, she reminded herself, not the secrecy afterwards. The secrecy was a gift. She *knew* this. It was her job.

Tomorrow, though, when William came home, she would sit him down and tell him the truth. *Ten years ago*, she'd say, *I had a month-long affair with Len Brice.*

If he was going to hear about it anyway, then

better from her. Better than from Len, whose recent indoctrination would have him speaking of *sin* and *betrayal.* Of *deliberate acts against the law of God.* No, Sandy would tell it for what it was. A little fun, a release, during a stressful time in their marriage. A mistake.

She hoped he'd understand. Short of that, she hoped he'd forgive her.

He called when his plane touched down in Columbus. The airport was just eight miles away. Full of nervous energy, Sandy had cleaned the house even though it was already clean. In the oven was the lasagna she'd made. In the refrigerator, spinach salad with walnuts and goat cheese. When he came home, they'd eat. Then they'd talk.

Now, she paced. She wanted a drink. Then she remembered about the snow boot. William didn't know that she kept a bottle of Scotch in her bedroom closet, inside the boot. She opened it so rarely now that the last time it snowed, several months earlier, she'd been surprised to find it there. She waited for ten minutes, looking out the front window as a car went by, then another. Then she went upstairs and rummaged around the floor of her closet looking for the boot. Took a small swig from the bottle. Replaced it in the boot, then went into the bathroom and brushed her teeth.

She looked into the mirror. "My marriage is going to end," she said, watching her own lips move, seeing what the words looked like. "Tonight my marriage is ending."

With a sponge, she wiped up a few shavings on the countertop from William's beard. Placed his tube of toothpaste in the medicine cabinet.

She listened for the electric garage door, for the too-hard slam of his car door, then, seconds later, the too-hard slam of the door leading into the kitchen. "I'm home!" he'd announce, like in a 50's sitcom.

She had gotten used to William. To the routine of

him. She loved him—maybe even more, all these years later, than she would have loved Bill. Because Bill would have stayed a child forever, and in time, she had to admit, he would have ended up becoming an irritation, a swollen appendix, while William had become as steady and warm and necessary to her as her own heart.

There was love between them. She felt it every day, beginning with the grapefruit he'd slice and sugar for her while she showered. And when they went to bed at night, he liked to take her hand and fall asleep without letting go.

The lasagna was beginning to burn.

The drive home from the airport took fifteen minutes, thirty in the heat of rush hour. But not fifty. Not ever fifty. She had already called his cell phone once, but hung up before leaving a voicemail. He hadn't called back. She turned the oven down to a low temperature. Something was wrong, obviously, but only in the barely conscious edges of her mind did the unthinkable take shape: Len meeting William at the airport. Waiting just beyond security to take him by the arm and guide him toward a seat so they could talk man to man. But the very thought was preposterous. Len would see William tomorrow morning when they came to work at 8:30 a.m. Surely that was soon enough.

She still had tonight.

And so she found herself thinking instead about the food she'd cooked, which was now overcooked—the scorched mozzarella, and the salad, no doubt becoming soggy in the refrigerator. She shouldn't have poured the dressing on until just before serving it, but she had. Why had she done that? Her palms were clammy. The ten years seemed gone, now, evaporated, and it was as if she were about to confess to something that'd just happened. As if the confession were making the affair real. Another swallow of Scotch would help, but she resigned herself to pacing. To inspecting corners of rooms for dust. To opening the oven door every few minutes to check on the state of things. Sixty minutes. You could drive halfway to Cincinnati in sixty minutes. Something was wrong—she could ignore the evidence for only so long—and she was about to call his cell again when the garage door opened, and then came the first door slam, and then the second, though before he could announce his presence she came into the kitchen to greet him, and how handsome he looked standing in the doorway with his suitcase and his computer bag, handsome in his coat and tie despite a day of travel, and before she could even cross the room, he said, "How could you?" as if the lie she'd been keeping filled up every single cell in his body, and then all of her plans fell apart, and she was nearly incoherent with half-sentences, with gasps and false starts, with sobbing, and her legs went weak and she was sitting down on the tile floor where there was no dust, not a single speck, repeating *I'm sorry* again and again while William looked on, stone-faced, still holding his bags, and the salad got ruined and the lasagna got ruined and everything got ruined.

He left again later that same night. Packed the suitcase with fresh clothes and went back out through the kitchen and into the garage. Sandy followed him from a distance. Walking by the trashcan, she noticed that the side had tomato sauce on it from when she'd dumped the dinner that neither of them was going to eat. By then over an hour had passed, and they'd moved from the kitchen into the living room, where from opposite ends of a long sofa she'd revealed everything. Not only the details, but, as far as she understood, the reasons: why the affair, why Len. And while she tried to explain these things so that the hurt would be minimized, she didn't try to sugar-coat them either. She told the truth. She explained her boredom with William all those years ago, and her self-loathing for being bored. She explained, too, why she hadn't told him before, how it'd just been that one affair. How, in her view, their marriage was good now. How she'd learned, over time, to love him all over again, and how it was real love, a full love, and how not a day went by when she didn't feel grateful for their life together now.

Sandy and William didn't fight often anymore, but in the early days of their relationship, before A.A., they sometimes had. Those fights usually had been sustained by whatever booze was in the house. And like the sex afterward, they had been loud and full of emotion.

Sandy wished that William would yell at her, or say something he couldn't take back. Yet all he did was ask curt questions, some with a tinge of sarcasm, but nothing more. He coughed out a few angry sobs, and then, when she stopped talking, he pursed his lips tightly as if stopping all the things he'd really like to say from escaping into the world. With his face damp and bright red, he went upstairs, unzipped his suitcase, and dumped it on the bed. Having said all there was to say, Sandy sat on a corner of the bed and looked on as he packed a set of clean clothes into the suitcase. When the suitcase was full, he zipped it and without another word went downstairs.

"Where are you going to sleep?" she asked when he'd reached the door leading to the garage.

William turned to look at her. "Don't worry about it."

"Will you be home tomorrow?" He hadn't packed much—just one suit, a couple of shirts, a few pairs of socks and underwear. She hoped this was a good sign.

He set down the suitcase. "How about you don't ask me any questions right now." He picked up the suitcase again and went into the garage.

Sandy followed him to the doorway. "William," she said. She knew she had no right to ask, but she was going to anyway. "You aren't going to go somewhere and . . . drink, are you?"

He watched her a moment, then turned around and

walked with his suitcase and computer bag to the car. He put the bags in the trunk, softly shut the trunk door, and got in the driver's seat. The garage door opened. He backed the car out of the garage and down the driveway, and was out of sight before the garage door shut again.

Two nights later, though, he was back. But not before Sandy bungled a case. Administrative assistant, fired after six months on the job. Now claiming a hostile work environment. Claiming that her supervisor, with whom she'd had a brief relationship, made her quit. The attorneys hadn't been called in yet. Everyone involved was hoping to head that off. Around the table sat the woman, her former supervisor, the company's director of human resources, and Sandy—who, incredibly, began the meeting by hearing herself say, "I feel as if there's hope for you two." Everyone's eyes widened.

"*Pardon* me?" The woman sat back in her chair and crossed her arms.

An hour later, nothing was resolved, and everyone seemed more frustrated than before the meeting had started. When Sandy got up and left, nobody thanked her. She wouldn't charge this company anything. She'd be lucky if she didn't get sued herself.

She'd barely slept the past two nights, and when she got home she thought she might take a nap. But she merely lay in bed, not falling asleep, while the sun set on the other side of the bedroom blinds and the room slowly darkened. She wasn't sleepy anymore, but there seemed to be no reason to get up. But after a while she must have fallen asleep, because suddenly the room was much darker, and she heard the garage door motor. She glanced at the clock—8:34—turned the light on, quickly splashed water on her face, and went downstairs to meet William.

He had his suitcase with him. That was good. And he looked haggard—shirt wrinkled, a bad shave. He looked like he needed her. His eyes, though, were sharp and clear. This was not a man with a hangover.

"You don't look too good," he said.

"I blew a case today." Immediately, she realized this was the wrong thing to say.

They went into the living room, sat together on the sofa and talked. They were calm about it, and Sandy learned things: that he'd always resented how little credit she gave him in his efforts at sobriety. That once, a number of years ago, he'd been tempted to sleep with a woman from A.A.

Sandy's stomach cramped up, hearing this. But she did her best to listen.

"I didn't go through with it," he said. "Even though you weren't there for me when I needed you. Even though she understood me better than you ever have, I didn't go through with it. That's the important difference."

"I wish you'd talked to me about it at the time," Sandy said.

"Yeah, well," he said, "I'm talking to you now. I don't think you really understand what it means for an alcoholic to quit drinking. What it's like having something like that over you every minute of every day." Sandy reached over and put her hand on William's, and as he talked, she rubbed the back of his hand with her thumb. "But I think it's important that you do know."

"I can try," she said. "I can do my best to understand."

"Did you really mean it when you said that you love me now?"

She said that she did.

He nodded, then looked at her a while. She let him look. Rubbed his hand with her thumb and waited.

And looking into her eyes, he said, "I'm going to cheat on you."

The rubbing stopped. "What do you mean?"

"You won't know when," he said. "Maybe in a year or two. Maybe longer. And when it's over, you won't know that either. But I'm absolutely going to cheat on you." She pulled her hand away and started to speak, but he cut her off. "Now, Sandy, give me a minute. I've thought this through. This is how it has to be. So that you'll know what it feels like."

"I *know* what being cheated on feels like. You don't have to—"

"No, that isn't it. This is how you'll know what *I* feel like. Every day. Waking up and wondering if today's the day when it all falls apart."

"That isn't fair," she said.

"I love you, Sandy," he said, "but it's completely fair. Believe me, I've thought this through for two days straight, and that's my offer. Take it or leave it. Your heavenly Father will never let you down. But I will."

He was asleep, his breathing deep and regular. He always slept well; maybe this was one reason why she hadn't known how much he still struggled. Sandy would wake up when William shut off the TV, or if a bird chirped too loudly, or whenever a motorcycle went past the house.

They had watched the eleven o'clock news, and then William had taken her hand, shut his eyes, and simply gone to sleep. Sandy looked at the TV screen. Letterman, then Craig Ferguson. When the news came on again, a repeat from earlier, she shut off the TV and listened to the near-silence all around her. Her watch ticking on the night table. A passing car. William, breathing.

He had presented a choice, but there had been no decision to make. She believed—she had to believe this; it was William's entire point—that every day was the first day. It never got easier. You only became better acquainted, through hard work, with your own weakness. But if every day really was the first, then she could make up for lost time. Starting tomorrow, she could be a better wife. She could learn to understand him better, help him more.

Or she could leave him. There was that option, too. Because no matter how she looked at it, that was one childish fucking ultimatum he had given her. It was mean, and manipulative, and unforgivable.

Or, it wasn't.

She wouldn't have believed it if she hadn't heard it herself. Nor was she convinced that he'd actually go through with his threat. She hoped he was lying. Hoped he was saying it because he believed it needed saying.

Unless he meant every word. That was also possible.

She moved her hand away from William's and got out of bed. The house was silent and chilly. She didn't know how to pray. She hadn't gone to church since being a child, and even then she hadn't liked it much. Still, she got on her knees by the side of the bed and put her hands together. But that reminded her of being in school, praying for an "A" while the exams were being handed back. So she dropped her hands to her sides and bowed her head, and she confessed not her sins but her powerlessness. Because that was the first step. She knew that much.

She felt uncomfortable, doing this—desperate, even a little stupid. But only a little. And less so the longer she sat there. She almost hoped that William would stir, catch her in this position, but he didn't. And when she was done, she got back in bed, under the covers, and felt around for his hand.

Training

All the Ashkenazi women were cutting off their breasts. I knew this was the proper word, though Andy Meltzer called them boobs and Ian Marcus called them tits and Ronnie Goldman called them cartons for a reason lost to me until he puckered up and mooed. On a sunny, cold fall day, I had stood in the Mount Sinai cemetery to watch my grandmother get buried. I remembered looking around at the nearby tombstones. My relatives going back two generations had paid in advance for a number of plots—for those now deceased as well as for those who hadn't gotten around to it yet. Looking at the dates, I was unsettled by all the people in my family who had died young. My grandmother's sister had been thirty-two. My mother's cousin had been forty-nine. Lifespans were shorter back then, I told myself, but this seemed excessive.

A year later, my father was sitting me and my sister, Michelle, down, my mother beside him, and together they told us about genes and Ashkenazi Jewish heritage, and Michelle said, "Jesus fuck," and I didn't know what to say, and anyway my mouth had gone dry, and all the chambers of my heart had collided. Finally, I squawked out a question: "What stage is it?" I had watched enough TV to know that cancer had stages. The higher the number, the worse it was. My father glanced over at my mother and said, "They don't really go by that anymore," which maybe was true, maybe not, or maybe it was true under some circumstances—but I knew damn well that if my mother's cancer were stage one, Dad would have said so.

That fall, my parents tried to keep me busy with scheduled activities: recreational sports and school jazz band and chess club. They encouraged me to go to the movies with my friends. I was in the eighth grade with increased independence but no wheels. Michelle, who had gotten her driver's license over the summer, carted me from place to place, the radio so loud that the speakers crackled in time with the bass drum. She had just tested positive for BRCA1 and BRCA2, which meant, she told me, that she'd won the cancer lottery with genes almost certain one day to turn her cells against her. "It's the only thing I ever won before."

Michelle, I should mention, was always the funniest one in my family, no contest. She had timing and wit on her side, not to mention a younger brother who was hopeless in the face of her attention. As a kid, she'd get me laughing so hard I'd have to leave the table so I wouldn't choke on my food. And if she started laughing first, forget it. But that was then. These days, her current repertoire was mainly gallows humor.

Today we were on our way to rec basketball training. They called it training rather than tryouts because everyone made a team. But the coaches needed to see everyone on the floor in order to divide the kids in a way that ensured league parity, or else the parents went nuts.

"So what are you gonna do?" I asked.

"Are you joking? The girls are as good as gone." I assumed she was talking about years in the future, decades, until she added, "So you're going to need a new chauffeur for a while."

"What are you talking about?"

"I'm talking about Christmas break."

"Chanukah," I said automatically.

She raised an eyebrow. "You think we get off from school for *Chanukah* break?"

I didn't like thinking about my sister's breasts. I had never thought about them at all until the day when Tony Andrews mentioned how big they were, and another kid was like, "Right. Duh," and it was the first time I really understood that people had conversations when I wasn't around to hear them.

"They won't do the ovaries until I'm older," Michelle said, "but the second I can do it, I'm doing it."

As we pulled into the Sportsplex parking lot, she told me about our older cousin, Sarah, who had also gotten tested and decided to have the procedures. And the woman from the pool, Mrs. Bloomberg, who had done it a couple of years back, and Jen, who sat at the front desk at Dad's law office. But all these women were older than Michelle. Jen didn't look much older than Michelle, but I knew she had a husband and a kid because I'd met them. I wondered when I was Michelle's age if I'd ever be as definite about anything. I couldn't even choose a sandwich.

"Don't you want kids someday?"

"I want a lot of things," she said. "What's your point?"

I felt stupid asking. "Don't you need ovaries to have kids?"

"Again," she said, "what's your point?"

We were rolling slowly past parked cars. She seemed to be looking for a spot even though all she had to do was drive up to the rec center and drop me off and then kill two hours before picking me up again.

"Can't you wait a few more years before going under the knife?" I had no idea where I'd heard that phrase, but I felt mature saying it.

My seat belt tightened as we lurched to a stop. The car behind us blared its horn. Michelle's dark green eyes locked on mine.

"I don't feel like having breast reconstruction and chemo at the same time, thank you very much," she said. "So no. It can't fucking wait."

This is the part that flashes ahead another year and returns us to the cemetery: same rabbi (now trying out a goatee), same family in attendance, many more friends—my mother made friends everywhere she went. It's another clear, blustery fall afternoon, the sky and trees an embarrassment of supersaturation. The Mourner's Kaddish ends, and people line up to shovel dirt onto the simple casket. Michelle is beside me—healthy, rebuilt, the ordeal of her own body now partly in the rearview. It isn't lost on her, will never be lost on her, that her brighter future, statistically speaking, is what has been salvaged from the wreckage of my mother's illness. In this moment in the cemetery, unable yet to begin processing the loss, I am no more than a receptacle for sensory stimulus. The sound of the dirt from my shovel as it lands on my mother's casket. The murmuring of the people waiting to return to their cars. The smell of pine needles. The sound of cars starting up. The sound of cars pulling away. My father, my sister, and I together. Somewhere far off, a leaf blower. A last look at the gravesite before we walk to the limousine provided by the funeral home. My limp, the result of an injury sustained almost exactly a year earlier, is almost gone. I'm standing between my father and my sister. They each place a hand on one of my shoulders.

Symmetry. The story is bookended. Or a chapter has ended. Or a new one has begun. Something about a book. I should have mentioned my mother was a reader.

◆ ◆ ◆

The car blared its horn again in the rec center parking lot, longer this time.

"So rude," Michelle muttered.

We went nowhere, Michelle having decided to test the limits of the other driver's patience. When the horn sounded again, she spun around in her seat and gave the other driver the finger. I turned my head and saw there was a boy in the front passenger seat of the car behind us, though I couldn't quite make out who it was. A second car came to a stop behind the car behind us.

Then a third car.

"What are you doing?" I asked.

"People should be decent to each other," she said. "It's literally the only thing that should be required of people."

Maybe so. Yet in the weeks since Mom's diagnosis, Michelle had been testing the bounds of decency and paying the price, with two in-school suspensions and a brush with the law. It was a small brush, but given the general law-abidingness of my family, Michelle seemed to me like a desperado. Braydon Kirkpatrick had been spreading rumors about her friend, Allie (I never did learn the specifics), and in retaliation, Michelle decided to toilet-paper the big oak outside his house. And not just with one roll, but dozens of them. The Kirkpatricks' house was set back from the road, and his family was out for the evening. Michelle had all the time she needed. She worked alone, without an accomplice or even telling Allie ahead of time. When she was done, the tree looked like a giant mummy had sprung free from its coffin. It would have been the perfect crime except for the surveillance camera that recorded the whole thing, making it the world's easiest bust.

Michelle sounded genuinely apologetic to the officer, to Dad and Mom, and, in the letter she penned and shoved in front of my face while I was trying to decode scientific notation, to Braydon's parents.

"Check out how sincere I can be," she said. I set aside my exponents. "I'm not legally required to write this," she explained as I read.

I handed her back her handwritten letter that was somehow both syrupy and confusing. *I have failed this test of my maturity and understand that in life there is no grade inflation.*

"I only apologized because Mom made me," she told me. "TP-ing a house isn't even vandalism in Delaware."

"You're lucky," I said.

"No, dummy." She tapped her head. "I do my research."

If so, then her research fell short. A few days after sliding her letter of apology into the Kirkpatricks' mailbox, Michelle got into trouble again at school (a day of in-school suspension) for barging into Allie's homeroom and calling her a fucking bitch in front of the whole class, then slamming the door and storming out. It turned out Allie had lied about Braydon spreading rumors about her. She was just mad because he'd asked another girl to homecoming.

I wondered now if we were about to be the victims of a road-rage incident in the parking lot of the rec center. I was fourteen and oblivious in some ways but not all of them. I knew we could get gunned down at any moment for any reason or for no reason at all. It seemed best not to make waves or pick fights with people we didn't already know well. I hoped Michelle wasn't expecting me to defend her. In gym class, I could barely bench-press the bar.

The car behind us decided to start emitting a single, sustained blast from its horn. Michelle sighed once, deeply. "Come on," she said. "Let's do this."

I didn't need to ask what she meant. She was already stepping out of the idling car. I obeyed her command—an automatic, younger-brother response having nothing to do with wanting to be her accomplice or saving her from herself or taking a risk on her behalf. I knew

Michelle was full of rage about Mom and about her own DNA, but I was full of terror. In the last couple of weeks, I had quietly quit jazz band and chess club. This was to no one's loss. I was a second-chair clarinetist who consistently failed to protect his queen. I came home and did my homework and played computer games and read books I'd already read a dozen times and stayed within proximity of my mother, who spent the afternoons working remotely from the guest bedroom—she was a freelance graphic designer—but really napping (wig on; the wig stayed on when there was even the remotest possibility Michelle or I might glimpse her) because the chemo and radiation wore her out. I knew it wasn't a treatment, either. Michelle had told me. It was an "experimental study," which, she explained, meant that someone someday might benefit, but it wouldn't be Mom.

When Mom woke up from her naps, she'd be groggy a while and then she'd be awake a while, puttering around the kitchen or maybe sitting on the sofa in the late-afternoon sun reading one of the books for one of her book clubs, and I knew there was literally nothing less important in the universe than jazz band or chess club—or rec basketball, but my parents had paid the league fee and the games were only once a week. I figured I'd start playing. I could always quit.

The man behind us in the parking lot, the man who could step out of his own car with a loaded gun if he wanted, he wasn't a man. He was just another high school kid a year older than my sister. Steve Collins. Steve's passenger was his younger brother, Milo, a sophomore.

"The fuck are you honking like that for?" my sister asked, but already her tone had shifted. She was playing it tough but wasn't angry anymore. We knew these guys. They lived in our neighborhood. There had been a couple of years, when we were all younger, that we'd gone to their house for Christmas dinner. Or maybe it was Christmas Eve. It was a long time ago. But there'd been a group of families from the neighborhood with kids of all different ages, and we'd sat around playing video games while the parents did parent things and the fire crackled in the fireplace.

"Aren't you too old for rec basketball?" my sister asked the younger brother, Milo.

"We're coaching," Steve said.

"Why?" Michelle asked.

"Volunteer points," Milo said.

I didn't like that answer. Points for what? If you volunteered for something, I thought, there shouldn't be points. Points made it not volunteering anymore because of the points.

But Michelle didn't seem put off. "Too bad for you," she said, giving Steve a look I hadn't seen on her face before, and it occurred to me that Steve's thick hair and stubble and height probably made him a good-looking guy. He grinned.

"Yeah?" he said. "Why's that?"

"Because you should blow it off," she said, as if the answer were as obvious as air or death or the first star of the night not being a star at all but rather Venus.

"What about me?" Milo asked. I figured he meant he didn't want his older brother to leave him to coach alone. But Michelle misunderstood, or maybe I did.

"It's not a date or anything," she said. "Come along if you want. Steve, park your stupid car. We'll hop in mine."

The line of vehicles by this point was backed up almost to the road. But Michelle didn't seem to be in any rush, and neither did Steve.

"Give us two minutes," he said.

"Sorry I gave you the finger," Michelle said.

"It's okay." He shrugged. "I get that a lot."

Fifteen minutes of riding silently beside Milo, while Michelle and Steve shouted to each other over roaring guitars, and the four of us were sitting on a small floating dock beside the kayak launch in Shadow Lake Park. The day was mild with sunlight shimmering off the water and brightening the leaves on the trees. Still, the sun this time of year never got high enough in the sky to convince you that daylight really meant it.

The lake was actually a shallow, brackish overflow of the bay. It had been years since I came here, yet after we arrived and threw a few pebbles into the water and settled on the floating dock, I began to feel the looming presence of the nearby train trestle and understood the reason we'd come here of all places. I couldn't have explained how I knew. It wasn't one thing, but a composite of all things: the last-gasp-of-fall weather; the line of cars; Michelle's new career as a delinquent; our chance encounter with two brothers who knew us from way back but not too well; Steve now being good-looking; the knowledge that death was approaching with the steady cruelty of a slow-moving freight train.

The trestle rose at least twenty feet above the lake. I knew kids who told rumors about other kids who'd crossed the trestle or jumped into the water, and I knew they were all lying. The lake couldn't have been more than three or four feet at its deepest, and only an idiot would traverse a trestle on an active rail line that was probably two hundred feet between ends. I knew all this, just as I knew, the way Michelle was glancing over at the trestle, that she was going to try.

"Don't," I said.

She looked at me. "Don't what?"

"Nothing," I said. "Just don't."

"I don't know what you're talking about," she said, standing up. She eyed the trestle again. "Do you know what, though? I feel like taking a walk."

"No!" I said. And then I added: "I have to take a leak." My bladder was fine. But if I reached the bridge first and started walking across, then she would see the idea for what it was, risky and stupid and selfish. And while I might have been three-and-a-half years younger, I was the faster runner.

Later, Michelle would insist she never meant to try to cross the trestle. She was only hoping Steve might take a walk with her so she could see what making out with him was like. That's what she would tell me, and her allegiance to her own story hasn't wavered. But I know what I knew.

I planned to step onto the trestle and go exactly as long as it took for Michelle to order me to turn around. She would see how dumb it was, and maybe she would see how dumb lots of things were that she was doing. Her behavior wasn't acceptable. I needed her. And I would continue to need her in increasing amounts because it was going to get awful. I knew that. But there was no telling her. I wouldn't find the right words, and even if I did, I knew she wouldn't hear them.

I also knew that my sister would never let me step onto that trestle. What I hadn't counted on, though, was Steve's distracting charm. Since when had Steve Collins become charming? Nor had I counted on Milo sensing that without my presence he was a third wheel and wandering off to the water's edge to spot killies.

Which was how I made it well over a third of the way across the trestle, one slow step at a time, before anyone saw me, and how the set of eyes didn't belong to Michelle or Steve or Milo but rather to the conductor of the slow-moving engine coming toward the trestle from the other side of the water. A full sprint and I could have made it back easily. But nothing was easy—because seeing the train, the enormous certainty of it, I found that my feet and legs had frozen.

The train blared its horn, and that's when I heard my sister. I didn't see her, couldn't look away from the train, but she didn't sound so far away.

"Jesus, Ben—fucking run!"

"I hate everything!"

My reply made no sense, yet Michelle seemed to understand. "I know," she yelled, "but turn around and run—now!"

"Fuck this!"

"Yes, Ben. Yes. Fuck this. Now run!"

"Fuck this!"

"Run!"

"Run, Ben!" Steve's voice. "Just turn around and do it!"

The train, though—it had me hypnotized. The steady *chug-chug-chug* over the tracks, the smell of oil, the engine's dark metal, the rust and dirt, the windows like a set of eyes. It looked like a grinning face. "I can't!"

"Then jump!" Michelle shouted. "Jump off the—" Her words were cut off by a long blast of the train's horn.

The trestle was too high. I knew that. "I can't!"

"Do it for me!" she shouted.

I would have. I would have done anything for her. But my feet might as well have been cemented to the tracks. I was rooted there, unable to do anything but watch the train come nearer until my world went painful and black. I saw that reserved plot of the cemetery, saw my own tombstone with that small span of years for some future kid to see and wonder about. Or no kid—because whose would it be?

The train blared its horn again, loud and scolding. I could already feel the impact. I was resigned to being next—me, not Mom—and it was as if Michelle heard my thoughts because she shouted, "Jump for Mom, Ben!"

Oh, how I wanted to. But I couldn't.

"Do it for all the Ashkenazi women!" she shouted.

Was she trying to be funny? Later, I would ask Michelle why she said it, and she would swear she had no idea—that she had simply barfed it out in desperation. But her absurd plea was what caused me to peel my eyes away from the train for a split second, long enough to break the spell, long enough for me to leap away and down into the shallow muck, and then, later—in the safety of her car, having dropped off the gone-silent Collins boys on the way to the emergency room to deal with my busted leg—for us to laugh until we cried, and to cry until we were somehow laughing again, and it went on like that, on and on, and even now, it's still going on.

Acknowledgments

First, second, and third, I must thank Kevin Watson for his ongoing presence in my life as editor and friend. Press 53 published my first collection of stories, and now, fifteen years later, they've published the one you hold in your hands.

There's no way to give enough thanks to the editors of the journals and anthologies where these stories first appeared—editors who said "yes," then got into the weeds to help make them better, then championed them once they were published—but I hope they know how grateful I am.

I'm grateful, too, to my colleagues/friends at Mississippi State University, where many of these stories were written. Thanks to the Delaware Division of the Arts for their support as well—the most recent stories were written in The First State (though not "The Highest Point in Delaware").

For their valuable feedback on these stories, special thanks to Christopher Coake, Michael Piafsky, Michelle Herman, and Becky Hagenston.

I'm very grateful to Phong Nguyen and Susan Perabo for reading the manuscript prior to publication and saying such kind things about it, and also for their own amazing stories.

And a big thanks to my family—the one I was born into, and the one I married into: I'm very, very lucky. Thanks to Sam and Wyatt, and of course to Katie, to whom this book is dedicated.

It's her, by the way. She's the highest point in Delaware.

Michael Kardos is the Pushcart Prize-winning author of six books of fiction, including the novel *Fun City Heist* and the story collection *One Last Good Time*. He is also the author of *The Art and Craft of Fiction: A Writer's Guide*. He lives with his family in Delaware.

www.ingramcontent.com/pod-product-compliance
Lightning Source LLC
LaVergne TN
LVHW050958080826
845145LV00009B/2340

* 9 7 8 1 9 6 8 7 8 3 0 2 0 *